Canky`s Trade

A Novel of Old Middleton

by John Wheatley

A Hulme Hall Publication

Copyright © John Wheatley 2013

PAPERBACK EDITION

`Canky`s Trade` is a work of historical fiction. Though the names
of some persons who once lived are used, their characterisation is
purely imaginative, and no actual resemblance is claimed.

Chapter 1

Byron - depressed, melancholic, at odds with the world - had kept to his chamber for three days. His lethargy seemed to have infected the whole house, though Burley, the manservant allocated to him – for he had brought none of his own – had discretely informed Robert Gregge Hopwood, whose guest the illustrious visitor was, that the gentleman had all but prevailed upon Flora, the chamber-maid, to part with her virtue, an outcome which had only been prevented by the sudden appearance of Lettie, the kitchen maid, who had brought the drink of water and vinegar which the gentleman had requested.

Not a gentleman, he reminded Burley, but a lord.

Lord George Gordon Byron, to give him his proper title. And certainly no gentleman, he muttered underneath his breath.

It was Lettie`s appearance that had brought Flora to a sense of her proper shame.

And so all was well.

Yes, said Robert Gregge Hopwood, thanking Burley and dismissing him. In truth, it was more likely that Lettie had been summoned for the same purpose as Flora, and that the two had, so to speak, cancelled each other out.

Still, it could have been worse, Hopwood admitted to himself. It could have been John, the fourteen year old trainee valet, or even worse, Derek, the stable lad.

He squeezed his eyes tight. All that sort of thing – or rather the loose talk and badinage which surrounded it - was all right at London and at Cambridge, but if all that sort of thing were to come out now, here in Middleton, at Hopwood Hall... well, it just wasn`t to be countenanced.

"Has he not yet concluded his business over Rochdale? asked Cecilia, Robert`s wife.

Byron`s purpose in coming to Lancashire had been to secure certain legal rights which pertained to the Manor of Rochdale.

Dear Robert, he had written, *I find I have, amongst the other diverse entitlements which my sad, bad and violent forbears have left me – Rochdale, which my immediate predecessor, a scurrilous villain, by all accounts, much like my father, attempted to mortgage or fraudulently sell. After my continental meanderings, I am in great need of the rents and other income it will furnish me with. Also, a project for a poem which I will enlarge upon when I see you. I propose a visit sometime in July.*

"Excellent," said Cecilia, full of initial enthusiasm. "We see little enough of the aristocracy hereabouts."

Then the visit had been postponed because of the sudden death of Byron`s mother. Hopwood had met her once, at Newstead Abbey, Byron`s own seat – a Gothic ruin only part of which had been renovated to be habitable. She was, as he reminisced to Cecilia, a very fat lady, who spoke with a Scots accent, drank heavily, and who had a tendency, in moments of exasperation, to make cruel jibes about her son`s limp. Byron himself, he recalled, when he had known him at Harrow and Cambridge, had a distinct tendency towards plumpness, though when he finally arrived in Lancashire, the Rochdale visit having been re-arranged for September, Byron, now twenty-three, and not long returned from his two years of travelling abroad, had become lean and spare, and with his curling auburn locks and striking eyes, was, especially to the women, an interestingly handsome fellow.

Cecilia, who had invited her two sisters, and a cousin, Mary Lovejoy, to meet their newly arrived guest, had been flattered when Byron declared himself in awe at the prospect of coming to a house so full of beautiful women, but then equally put out when he said he would not come down to dinner that night because it was his `fasting` day. It was Mary Lovejoy, somewhat older than her cousins, who went to speak to him, warning him of the dangers of taking only vinegar and water, and who persuaded him at last to accept the hospitality which had been prepared for him.

The mood had been a little awkward, at first. When Eleanor, Cecilia`s younger sister, ventured to tell Byron, who was sitting somewhat languidly in his chair, that she had read *Hours of Idleness*, the volume of poems Byron had published before going abroad, Byron replied by saying that he would *endeavour by all means possible to devise a programme of activities in which she might spend her time more profitably,* there was some uncertainty as to whether his irony was of the self-deprecating kind or a jibe belittling the young lady. "What I mean to say," Byron continued, sensing that he had struck the wrong note, "is that I shall attempt to make any further ventures in the field of verse more worthy of the young lady`s kind attention."

A quiet sigh of relief was collectively breathed.

"You have already, if I`m not mistaken," said Mary Lovejoy, in the manner of one who was seldom mistaken about anything, "had published some verses of a satirical nature."

"That is true," said Byron, "though it will be revised, or withdrawn. Some people have been pleased to call it clever, but cleverness is no substitute for truth."

"Will you not," said the younger sister, glad that her knowledgeable elder cousin had been silenced, "write of your travels abroad. I am given to believe, from Robert, that you have visited some strange and very exotic places."

"In truth, I have..." said Byron, now beginning, like an actor on the stage, to warm to his role.

And after that, the evening had been a complete success. Portugal, and the marvels of Cintra, in its cradle of rocky crags, the mountains of Albania and time spent at the court of the Ali Pasha of Iannina, Constantinople, Greece, noble in her ruins, and so it went on.

Cecilia had been as enthralled as everyone else. He had seen, glancing sideways, that look of rapt attention on her face that one usually associates with children being told a particularly magical tale. For a brief time, Robert congratulated himself that the visit of his erstwhile fellow at Trinity was to be, socially speaking, a coup de grace!

"We must arrange a soiree, even a ball," Cecilia said, making an inventory of the families who made up the gentry of the surrounding country: the Ashtons of Alkrington; the Radcliffs of Foxdenton; the Hortons of Chadderton; the Starkies of Heywood and Tonge. Possibly Lady Mary Assheton of Middleton Hall, who now lived there alone, her husband, Lord Suffield having recently died, and her two sons being in London or Norfolk. Lady Mary had something of a reputation for being ill-tempered, but she would have to be invited. In all likelihood, she would excuse herself, anyway, so all was well. Then there was Ezekiel Barton, the new industrialist, as her husband called him, with his wife and daughters and son. It had somehow become *de rigeur* to have Barton at social events, these days.

Cecilia had been, he fancied, along with her younger sister, a little infatuated with Byron.

She thought differently now.

"These things take time," said Robert, responding apologetically to her question regarding Rochdale. Byron had brought his solicitor, Hanson, with him to the north, to act as his advisor and agent, but Hanson had been delayed in Manchester. "There are legal niceties."

"They take time when you stay abed all day for three days," she said emphatically. "There are no legal niceties about that."

"His mother died suddenly, remember, it`s not surprising if his spirits are affected..."

"I thought you said he didn`t even like her."

"To like not is not necessarily to love not," said Robert, surprising even himself with this profundity.

6

Cecilia drew in a long breath, ill disguising her impatience, but said no more.

He rather suspected that Burley`s impeccable discretion had been circumvented by others and that a version of the tale of Flora and Lettie  had reached Cecilia`s ears.

"I`ll have a word with him," said Robert, meekly.

"Good. And make it a sharp one."

And that was that.

"It`s this damnable Lancashire weather," said Byron. "A shower of rain enlivens the imagination, a morning mist quickens the spirit, but for it to go on incessantly for three days, like this, sodden, miserable - that is just an oppression to the soul."

"It is not always so," said Robert, trying to introduce a lighter tone, though the forlorn prospect from the window persuaded him not to risk an encomium on the variety and temperateness of the local climate. "It must have been very different in Spain and Albania," he added instead.

"That`s true, Robert. It is. The sun is a great beautifier. The southern tribes worship the sun. The northern tribes worship the forest, I think."

"Though we are all united in common worship of a Saviour," said Robert, immediately aware, as Byron stifled a yawn, of how trite it sounded.

"I have been remiss," said Byron, suddenly, decisively, standing and moving across the room with his characteristic slight limp, towards the window. "I have ill repaid your splendid hospitality, and more especially that of your charming wife. I will make amends."

"Please," said Robert, "there is no..."

Byron held up a silencing hand.

"I will make amends."

"If you wish, let me accompany you to Rochdale tomorrow. If Hanson is further delayed, I will put my solicitor, Banks, at your disposal. Excellent man, Banks."

"I`ve heard that there is a church of some note in these parts," Byron ventured, without answering the proposal.

"In what particular aspect?"

"A church with a wooden steeple."

"Ah, St Leonard`s, in Middleton."

"St Leonard, the patron saint of thieves. I`m intrigued."

"Well, then. Let`s pay it a visit, if that`s your inclination."

"Excellent. Thank you, Robert, I`m in a better mood already."

It was with some misgivings that Robert carried this good news to his sceptical wife, but to his relief she was sufficiently appeased to send Burley to ask their visitor if he would care to join them at supper, and the reply he brought back was in the affirmative.

Chapter 2

Canky`s wife was in the middle of what Canky called one of her shrewish fits, and when she was in the middle of one of those, an energy was at work which was pointless to resist.

If Canky had been out until three in the morning – which he had - without coming come home drunk – which he wasn`t – it meant, according to Canky`s wife, that he had been with another woman.

Or more than one woman.

"Since I`ve never known you last more than three minutes, at the best of times, and there haven`t been that many of them, you could have been with half a dozen and still had five hours to spare, for all I know."

The shrillness of her voice could be heard in all the neighbouring houses, but they were used to it.

Canky waited patiently to defend himself.

The amazing thing, and all the neighbours agreed with this, was that Canky had managed to get such a young wife at all. He`d been married before, of course, and when they carried her coffin to the grave, they said it was the lightest they`d ever carried.

"She held on for so long," said Canky, "There was little more than the skeleton left in the end."

Canky was forty, and he had a skinny wiry body, and a reddish nose, because there was no argument that he`d done a fair amount of drinking in his time, but, somehow, he always seemed to have some money in his pocket.

The present Mrs Canky, who, at eighteen, when she met him, had been a pretty thing with pink cheeks and a plump bosom, and who now, at twenty four, was a handsome woman still, must have been seduced, common rumour went, by the money in his pocket. It was a well-known fact that her own family had none, and that after her marriage, her mother had been able to live – albeit for a very short time – and then die, in comfortable circumstances.

"I was engaged in business," said Canky, when at last the shrewish fit subsided.

"What business does a sexton have, tell me, until three o`clock in the morning?"

"We`re on the look-out for these resurrection men," said Canky. "We have to stay up and look out for them."

"Well, why didn`t you say so?"

"I didn`t want to upset you, with tales of bodies and such like."

"Are you telling me true?" asked Mrs Canky, softening in the way she always did after her shrewish fit had subsided.

"Look," said Canky, "I`ve got you this." He produced from his pocket a grubby looking handkerchief which he unfolded to reveal a fine silver chain. In fact, the chain had been intended not for her but for a silversmith of his acquaintance who would give him a good price, but in the circumstances, he considered the decision to make a gift of it well-judged.

The look on Mrs Canky`s face confirmed that this was so.

"You do love, me Canky, don`t you?"

"How can you doubt it?"

"Here let me try it on, and bring me the glass so I can see."

"Now, my little Jenny Wren, you look like a princess and it`s no less than you deserve, but mind, I don`t want you parading this in public, lest people get wind that Canky`s got deeper pockets than he truly has, and break in at night and murder us and rob us to get their hands on such little trinkets as this."

"I won`t," she said, with as much earnestness as she could muster, and Canky was sure that she would stick to her part of the bargain.

"One day, we`ll move away from here to somewhere where we don`t fear being murdered and robbed in the middle of the night, and then you can go about in all your finery, but until then..."

"Mum`s the word."

"That`s it, Jen. And now, I think I`ll take to my bed for an hour, and if you`re a grateful and obliging wife, you might feel inclined to join me there."

"I do," said Jenny Canky. "I am so inclined."

"Well, then let`s talk about it no more, but make haste."

"But not too much haste, I hope, Oliver," she said leading the way up the stairs.

"Get away with you, hussy," he said, slapping her bottom playfully as he followed. "I`ll make what haste I please!"

A neighbour at her hand-loom, formed the momentary impression, ten minutes later, that the shrewish fit had resumed, but then, with a wry smile, realised her mistake.

Chapter 3

"**H**eaven be praised!" muttered Robert Gregge Hopwood, when, peeping through the curtains of his chamber window, he saw the benign rays of morning sunlight filtering through the woodland trees which formed the view.

He summoned Baines, his valet, and was quickly dressed. Descending the staircase, he was met by Burley who informed him that his lordship had risen early and had left the house with the intention of bathing in the river.

"More madness for a May morning!" muttered Robert, between his teeth, as he set out in the direction of the brook, two hundred yards from the Hall. The driveway from the Hall passed over a stone bridge where the river beneath widened and formed a shallow pool, with a bank of shale and sand, and it was as he approached this spot, that he heard, even before he saw him, the sound of Lord Byron`s sport, a mixture of splashing and high-pitched whooping which expressed both the pleasure and the sharp coldness of his exploit.

"What are you doing, man?" said Robert, laughing. "You`ll catch your death of cold."

"You are talking," said Byron, "to a man who has swum across the Hellespont. Come and join me."

"Not on your life!"

"`Hero and Leander`, remember it?"

"On Hellespont, guilty of true-love's blood,
    In view and opposite two cities stood..."

"You`ve got it. Now what about the rest?"

"What do you mean, the rest? I thought that was it."

"You Philistine. Sestos and Abydos. Now, pass me that towel, take your eyes off my withered leg, and feast them on my excessively diminished genitalia."

"I will avert my eyes."

"What a place!" said Byron, when he had dried himself and put on his shirt and breeches.

"It`s pleasant, is it not?" said Robert.

"Pleasant is not the word for it. It`s magnificent. Some very English poet should come and extol its beauties."

"Perhaps yourself?"

"No, not me. My old friend Turdsworth might do, though you might have to stick a couple of mountains in the background, to get him keen on it."

"I take it you mean the celebrated Mr Wordsworth."

"That`s what I said, isn`t it, the celebrated Mr Turdsworth?"

"You`re in good spirits. Let`s go back and have some breakfast."

"I`m not hungry yet. I want to see more of your estate. Where is the new canal?"

"Less than a mile, but let`s eat, for I`m hungry if you`re not, George. Then I will have two horses saddled and I will show you the estate."

"Very well. Let it be so."

The Rochdale canal, the first to cross the Pennines, linking Liverpool, Manchester and Leeds, was opened in 1804, after twenty years of wrangling between different companies, proposal and counter-proposal, progress, delay, and section by section construction.

"The problem is over the summits," explained Robert, who, as a youth had felt his own father`s enthusiasm for the project, and had accompanied him to see the vision, almost biblical, of hundreds of navvies digging out the course of the canal, shovel by shovel.

They were standing, on horseback, by the Slattocks lock, having made their way from the hall through Lord`s Wood, past the corn mill and the mill race.

"The summits," said Byron. "Explain that."

"It's to do with the water supply. You see this barge which is now approaching the lock. As they enter the lock, they will close the gate behind, and then open the sluice to bring the water levels together."

They watched as this operation was completed, and then as the upper lock gates opened and the barge moved on.

"Magnificent," said Byron. "Such simplicity, and yet such genius to translate simple scientific laws into such a machine."

"As for the summits," said Robert, "as you can imagine, the steeper the gradient, the greater the number of locks required, and from this, the problem of the supply of water."

"I see," said Byron. "From what I have seen so far, I wouldn't have thought that the supply of water in these parts would be a problem, but I take your point."

"The Huddersfield link is the shortest route, but that depends on tunnelling, and so far that is still an incomplete work."

"Fascinating," said Byron, without irony.

They stayed to watch as another barge approached the lock in a different direction, and then another. The fresh morning had turned now into a cloudy noon, but the air was still warm and fragrant, and there was no threat of rain.

"And now," said Byron, "your church of St Leonard. I am impatient to see it.

"So, you shall," said Robert, drawing on the reins, and turning his horse. "So you shall."

Chapter 4

After a good two hours' morning rest, Oliver Canky made his way along Lodge Street to Market Place, where he had certain matters of practical business to transact, and people to meet, and then he continued to the Old Boar's Head, where he met with three fellows who were able to confirm that a certain piece of business, begun the previous evening, had been successfully completed.

"Good work, lads," he said. "I'll meet you here tonight, and we'll see what further matter is to do."

"A couple of night's rest wouldn't go amiss with me," said one.

"I'm not complaining," said another, "As long as the trade's good and it puts money in my pocket..."

"I didn't say I was complaining. I just said a night's rest..."

"You'll get your rest tonight, Ned," said Canky, clapping him amicably on the shoulder. "Here take this florin and bring in some drinks."

Leaving the Boar's Head, he watched the midday stage coach pass, labouring slowly up from Market Place on its way to Thornham and Rochdale, and then made his way across the paddock towards St Leonard's church perched on the brow of the hill above.

"Quiet night, Mr Canky?" enquired the church warden, as he approached.

"Quiet night," replied Canky. "There'll be no resurrectionists hereabouts whilst Oliver Canky has breath in his body."

"Have you money to pay the men of the watch?"

"They do it from good will, in the main, though I sometimes let them have a few coppers so that they have something to take back to their families."

15

"Here," said the warden handing a small pouch of coins.

"No need," said Canky, holding up a hand.

"Take it," said the warden. "Mustn`t have you out of pocket."

"Thank you, sir."

"Now," said the church warden, proceeding to the business for which he and Canky met each day. "There`s the collier`s wife from Woodfield Row, but that`s a family plot, so it`ll just need to be opened and made decent. Then there`s the crippled son of the blacksmith Dyson. That`ll need to be ready for Thursday."

"Right," said Canky.

"Good man," said the warden. "How`s Mrs Canky? Well, I hope?"

"Very well, sir. At least she was when I last saw her, an hour since, very well indeed."

"Glad to hear it. And now I must get about my business, and delay you no longer."

"Thank you, sir," said Canky, tipping his cap respectfully, and making his way to the small door in the church wall which opened on the store where his tools were kept.

By now the midday coach from Market Place to Thornham and Rochdale had reached the hamlet of Stannycliffe, and it was here that it was passed by two horsemen approaching from the other direction. One, the coachman recognised as the squire of Hopwood, the other he had not seen before, though a certain hauteur of face and bearing bore witness, as did his garments, to his being a gentleman of some standing. Taking the reins in his left hand, he took his hat off with his right hand, and made, so far as was compatible with his position and the safety of his passengers, an obeisance.

The Squire nodded in acknowledgment, the stranger ignored him, and the coach passed on.

"There is a smell of coal smoke," said Byron, as they approached the first rows of houses on the northern outskirts of the village of Middleton.

"Yes," said Robert, "there is a scattering of collieries in the countryside hereabout, and a decent trade in coal."

"I`m informed that there are coal seams in my Rochdale estates."

"Indeed."

"And Middleton is so called because…?"

"If you follow the routes from the townships of Bury and Rochdale to Manchester, you would find Middleton in a roughly central position."

"It sounds very sensible," said Byron. "Very English."

They rode on for a further quarter of a mile in silence, Robert feeling somewhat piqued by his friend`s condescension. When they reached the brow of St Leonard`s, however, progressing by Cheapside and Barrowfield, it was clear that his old friend and fellow alumni of Cambridge, was truly impressed.

The church of St Leonard commanded a panoramic view of the surrounding countryside, comprising farm and woodland, rising gently, on one side, to the heights of Oldham and the moors beyond, and on the other to the near hills of Langley, Hebers and Birch.

"Over there," said Robert, "just beyond that clump of trees, you can see Tonge Hall."

Byron nodded, acknowledging the view.

Below them, at the corner of the graveyard, the sexton was at work digging a grave.

"Canky," said Robert. "Oliver Canky. The sexton, a good man."

"Let us approach and see his work."

Canky looked up, his face red with sweat, and wiped a rag across his brow.

"Sirs," he said.

"Good day, Canky," said Robert.

"Alas, poor Yorick," said Byron.

"Don`t tease him," said Robert.

17

"I knew him Horatio," said the sexton, unexpectedly.

"Bravo," said Byron.

"We sextons know our own literature," said Canky. "It's not an extensive one, but it suffices for such moments as this."

"You're an excellent fellow, Canky," said Byron. "Here's a crown for you," he added, tossing a coin in the sexton's direction, "if you can pick it out of the grave you dig."

"If I don't, there's others who will, sir."

"Then take it, man," said Byron turning his horse's head away, back in the direction of the church.

The southern aspect of St Leonard's Church gave out, beyond the gate and the immediate churchyard, onto a rough meadow, called the Warren, grazed by sheep. It extended for fifty yards and then dipped away steeply on three sides, looking down over the shambles and the market place, and, to the left, over the extensive grounds of Middleton Hall, the seat of the Assheton family.

The hall was set amidst avenues of trees, with formal gardens to one side, and, just beyond, a lake fed by a branch of the river which curved around the parkland with three wooden footbridges crossing to the meadows on the other side.

"I've heard the name of Assheton," said Byron. "An ancient family?"

"Yes. Sir Richard Assheton led the Middleton Archers at Flodden Field. There is a window in the church commemorating the event."

"And the family live there still?"

"The male line ended a generation ago. The eldest daughter of the last baron married Lord Suffield."

"Ah, Lord Suffield..."

"Who, as you may know, died this last year."

"No, I did not. Lord Suffield was primarily of Norfolk, was he not?"

"Indeed, and the family spent a great deal of time there, much more there, in fact, than here, though Lady Mary, Lord Suffield`s widow, lives here now."

"Perhaps, I should call and pay my respects."

"I`m sure that would be…"

"Not now though," said Byron, cutting in sharply. "But some other day, perhaps."

"Certainly."

They turned their horses back towards the church.

"I should like to ride by here at night," said Byron. "To see how this aspect looks under the moon and the stars."

"Really?" said Robert Gregge Hopwood, trying to conceal his lack of enthusiasm, though sensing that Byron would have his way if he so wished it.

"Yes," said Byron, with a hint of the mischievous glee which reminded Robert of his friend in younger days, setting about hare-brained schemes, "I`m rather fond of the night."

Robert smiled, hoping that it was a whim which would be quickly forgotten, as they rode back towards the church of St Leonard, with its distinctive wooden steeple and crenelated walls.

Chapter 5

In the Old Boar's Head, the same evening, a young weaver, Samuel Bamford, was telling the group of men who surrounded him of the exploits of his father, a wrestler and fist-fighter of some notoriety, though otherwise a decent law-abiding and god-fearing man.

"Aye, with all the wild rough fellows of the neighbourhood, either here, in the threshing bay of this very house, or at the Church Tavern up the hill there," he continued, "when the mood was on him, he drank and danced, and when nothing else would do he fought with the moodiest and the merriest of them!"

"Was he a rhymester, too, like you Sam? Did he stand up on the table and churn it out like you do?"

"I'll tell you what," said Sam Bamford, "they made him master of the manufactory at the Salford Workhouse and he whisked the whole lot of us down there and that put a stop to his fighting days!"

Bamford was not drunk, but he was warmed with ale, though not so much as with the warmth of his own performance. He was a natural story-teller, a man who had the talent to silence those around him, and to command their attention.

His colourful performance, and the mirth and ribald retorts which it occasionally provoked, was a convenient distraction to a small group of men sitting in the furthest shadowy corner of the room, talking quietly under the fog of their own pipe smoke.

"A cripple, you say?" said one, not, judging from his accent, a local man, and wearing a scarf which partly covered his face.

"Yes," said Oliver Canky, who made one of the group. "No use?"

"Far from it. What was the cause of his affliction, birth or accident?"

"Born a cripple."

"Even better."

"Then maybe we should talk of business?"

A great ripple of laughter, spreading across the room, distracted them momentarily.

"The usual fee," said the man with the scarf, as the laughter abated.

"In this case, being the offspring of a poor blacksmith, and there being no, how shall we say, extras...."

"The usual fee."

"...and if his condition is of particular interest..."

"You drive a bargain, Mr Canky. Very well, the usual fee, and three guineas in addition. If it sits with your conscience."

"You tell us we do the world a service, and that we weigh in the balance of our consciences, but we do not do this work lightly."

"I do not doubt it."

"Good,"

"So, when will this be?"

"Tomorrow, or the next night."

"Very well."

The man with the scarf rose, and slipped two florins onto the table. "That is for your further refreshment," he said. "I'll leave now, before this local fool has done. Send me word, and you'll be met at the usual place."

Sam Bamford, his larger audience now dispersed, was talking to a smaller group of cronies in the corner opposite. He had a fund of stories. Middleton born, he had moved away, as he was fond of telling people, when his father was appointed at the Salford Workhouse. He had received a decent education in Manchester, was a great reader of books, and had - before returning to Middleton at the age of twenty, and marrying his childhood sweetheart, Mima - worked as a warehouseman, a weaver, even as a sailor on the merchant line from Hull to London – from which he had absconded – and that made another of his colourful tales. He had been subjected to some temptations and had resisted them. He had been subjected to others and had not.

He was telling them now, that one morning, not many years ago, after a youthful misdemeanour committed by himself during a night of revelry, near Christmas time, he had flung himself on the bed and had been wakened just at breaking day by a rough voice which he recognised as that of Samuel Fielding, the constable.

"Well, he was asking for my uncle, at whose house I was staying, but I had a shrewd idea it was me he was after. A powerful broad-set man he was too, and he was standing with his back against the door post, holding the door catch with one hand. `Does one Samuel Bamford bide here?` he asked, and I could tell from that, what with the shutters being still closed and the place quite dark, that he hadn`t made out who I was. `He`s upstairs,` I said, `but I can call him down if you want him.` And with that I went to the foot of the stairs, and called up, lustily, `Samuel! Come down, thou`rt wanted.` And I said to the constable, `you`d better step in and sit down. He`ll be here in a minute.` The cunning old fox, though, would neither come in nor sit down; so I loitered about in the dark, humming a snatch of a tune, and shuffling to and fro, betwixt the house and the kitchen. I heard some of the family stirring, obviously mystified at me calling up to summon myself, and so I said to the constable, `he`ll be here directly, he`s coming,` and with that I shot the bolt of the back door, and darted out and down the street, never stopping to look at the other constable waiting outside who made a grasp at me, and the wind of whose fist, as I sprung past him, I felt on my ear. I leaped over the fence in the lane, and ran off with this new foe at my heels. He chased after me, and fast he was too, but he might as well have been chasing the hart-royal, and by the time he`d got back, puffing and blowing, to the bottom of my uncle`s stairs, I was safe in Middleton Wood..."

When his tale was done, and as the company began to thin out, Bamford sat back, and with his pot of ale settled on his lap, looked contentedly towards the fire. It`s now a question, he said to himself, of whether to have another one or not.

Samuel Bamford knew the pleasures of drink, and he also knew its excesses, excesses which could draw with them other vices as fascinating in the moment of temptation as they were shameful to contemplate afterwards. Well, he said to himself at last, I'll have a last one to set me off in the way of sleep, and a nice slow pipe to accompany it. He might have called out to be served where he sat, but being in the way of needing some space in his bladder to make room for his last tipple, he made his way out into the yard, and on his way back in stood at the bar to avoid any waiting for service.

It was as he stood there, that his eye, drifting this way and that, suddenly came to rest on another pair of eyes belonging to one who was sitting in the corner of the little snug room by the door. I know those eyes, he said to himself. And at the same time, those eyes, looking back at him, seemed to be saying, and I know your eyes, too, Sam Bamford. I know your eyes, too!

They were green eyes, as green and subtle as a cat`s eyes. And despite the shabbiness of her garments, and the hard and ill-used look of her face, and despite the bruise under her left eye, the eyes were green and subtle still. Quite unmistakeably, though not seen in Middleton for five years, or more, they were the eyes of Lucy Brindle.

Chapter 6

But the Brindles were Middleton folk, honest, decent hard-working Middleton folk. Her father was a collier and her mother ran two looms at the cottage they had in Boarshaw. When Sam came across Lucy for the first time, they had both been sent from their homes to bring milk from the dairy at the foot of Hollin Lane, and it was reckoned then that the family were doing well, with their two trades, better than most. Lucy was then a spirited girl of twelve and Sam was thirteen, lanky and clumsy as he thought himself, and awkward and tongue-tied, especially with girls. But he had fancied himself in love with her, Lucy Brindle, with her gooseberry green eyes, and as he lay abed, he had begun to compose his first verses, extoling her beauty and her virtue, as he thought a poet should, and linking one to the other, as he also thought he should.

Then, his father shifted the family to Salford, and after that he only heard scraps, when he came back to visit his uncle and aunt, of people he had known in his Middleton days. The Brindles, he heard, had been overtaken by bad luck and had fallen on hard times. Old Tom Brindle, Lucy`s father, had been killed in a pit-fall, and her elder brother, Jem, had enlisted and died from the typhus fever in Spain. Mrs Brindle, Lucy`s mother, had let her looms go badly so that no-one would trust her with work, and the last Sam heard at that stage was that the family had quit the area altogether.

Some said they had other family in Yorkshire, and Sam hoped that was true, but he didn`t think about it for long. His life was too busy and full to brood long on things gone by. He had discovered Alexander Pope`s translation of the Iliad, and he had discovered his beloved Milton, and despite his humble occupation as a warehouseman, his imagination was full of the sense of glorious and romantic things.

24

One night, high in mirth, well into his cups, he had become separated from his drinking companions, young scoundrels all, as they cavorted and played chase-and-run amidst the midnight backstreets of Manchester, near the old Church and Long Mill. At last finding himself alone, and being sensible enough to realise that it was time he wended his way home, he found himself suddenly in the company of a young woman who had slipped her arm through his and was asking him for protection back to her lodgings, for fear of a gang of ruffians who, she said, had been bating her. His tired spirits rallying, and full of bravado, he assured her that she would be seen home safe, if he had anything to do with it, and it was not long before he began to realise, from her blandishments, that the young woman had intentions for him other than those of seeing her safely to her door-step.

Indeed, it was not to a door-step that she led him, but to the top of an alley lit only by moonlight, and it was here, in a riotous confusion of feeling, that he found himself in danger of succumbing to her soft persuasions. And might have done so, too, had he not suddenly recognised, under the light of the moon, the gooseberry green eyes of Lucy Brindle.

He had pressed a half-crown into her hand, and begged her forgiveness.

"Don`t leave me like this, Sam," she pleaded, as he ran away down the alley. "Don`t leave me like this."

At the bottom of the alley, a large brutish fellow was waiting. "That was quick," he said. "What`s going on?"

"Get out of my way."

"Too bloody quick for my liking. If you`ve not paid her, you can pay me."

"I`ve paid her," said Sam.

"Then you can pay me as well, since you seem to have baulked at the goods."

"Get out of my way," said Sam, again.

"And will you make me?" said the brute.

25

Sam left him, not long after, measuring his length along the pavement.

But it took him many days of prayer and repentance, and many nights of troubled thought, to begin to forget the terrible vision, in the moonlight, and in a dark stinking Manchester alley, of the gooseberry green eyes of Lucy Brindle.

And now, in the corner of the snug room of the Old Boar`s Head, as he was waiting to be served, he was looking at those eyes again.

Chapter 7

"**C**ome and have a drink with me Sam, for old time's sake!"
"What are you doing here, Lucy?" he said, going over to sit beside her before anyone noticed, the less to make any fuss.

"A've come home," she said.

"Who gave you that bruising about your eye?"

"Yon chap. You know the one. He'll not be looking for another bout wi' you the way you dealt wi'im last time."

Sitting opposite her now, Sam Bamford observed that though her eyes still had some of their old allure, the flesh of her cheeks had become roughened and coarse, and her once rich nut-brown hair had become lank and dry. They were symptoms he had seen before in people for whom the consolations of the bottle had become habitual.

"Have you come to visit someone, Lucy? Do you still have people hereabouts?"

She shook her head, and took out a small clay pipe, asking him if he could oblige her with a few shreds of baccy, which he did.

"Have you somewhere to stay?" he asked, with an uncomfortable feeling that his ticklish conscience was leading him into obligations which he was far from wanting to uphold.

"Why, are you going to put me up toneet wi' you and yours, Sam Bamford?"

He began to mumble an apology, but seeing immediately from the satirical look in her eye that she meant no such thing, he felt both embarrassment and relief.

"I'm looking for a gentleman called 'owarth," said Lucy. "Had some business with me a while back over in Greengate, and he said as I might come and see him here anytime, as we

27

both hailed from the same town, only like a proper gentleman, he didn`t tell me exactly where he lived."

"Howarth," said Sam. "It`s not an uncommon name, and you know how scattered the homesteads are."

"You`ve just brought him to me, Sam, Owd Scat, his cronies called him, his drinking cronies. Owd Scat, or Scrat, it might have been. They`d had some business on the river t`neet before, and had money burning holes in their pockets."

As soon as Lucy mentioned this soubriquet, Sam Bamford knew exactly the man she was talking about. Indeed, he could have told her that the man who went by that name had been part of the little group thick in conversation with Oliver Canky not an hour ago, when he had been enjoying his own bit of sport with the other fellows in the tap room; indeed, he could have told her that the same man was still in there, as far as he knew, or at least had been up to the point where he`d gone out into the yard to relieve himself.

Owd Scrat lived in an old rambling and dilapidated house up on the church brow, at the far corner of the Warren, not far from the vantage point from which, earlier in the day, Squire Hopwood, as he was known locally, and his visitor had looked out over the scene below. It was a solitary house, sheltered by high trees and overlooking the market place and the hall, so that if the town had wanted to set up a watch tower to spy on its own business, secret or otherwise, that would have been precisely the place to put it. It was perhaps for that reason that Owd Scrat had something of an unsavoury reputation for being where he could see and hear other people`s business without being seen or heard himself. More than one young woman, it was said, careless of her chamber shutters at nightfall or in the morning, had reported becoming aware of the patient and attentive gaze of Owd Scrat, but these reports were second-hand, for indeed, what father would allow his daughter - or what husband his wife – to make gossip out of her own carelessness when getting dressed or undressed?

Another story had it that Owd Scrat had murdered his wife, and boiled her up in a vat until all the bones came loose like those of a chicken rendered down for stock, but in fact Scrat had never been married, and so had never had a wife to consider murdering, in the first place.

They also said that he was a resurrection man, digging up bodies and robbing graves, but as far as Sam Bamford was concerned these were stories perpetuated by children with over-eager imaginations, or by folk who would make up anything to have a lugubrious tale to tell - and Scrat, living alone, as he did, and in a lonely spot, was the kind who attracted such tales. He was not one who Sam had much conversation with, and he had no reason to feel any friendly or neighbourly inclinations towards him, but the truth was that he knew no actual harm of him.

Which left him with something of a dilemma. Was he to say nothing, and leave Lucy to fend for herself, and sleep rough, as she probably would; or was he to lead her directly to an unsuspecting fellow for whom the introduction might well be as unwelcome as it was unexpected?

"I think I know the man you mean, Lucy," he said at last. "He sups here, sometimes, and sometimes at the Assheton Arms, and other places in the town. But if you wait by the stile, across the way from here, that`s the way he`ll pass, on his way home, if he`s about at all."

"Thank you, Sam," said Lucy. "And now, for sentimental reasons, and because I was once as sweet on you as you were on me, buy me a nice drink to keep me warm, through the night, whatever might come of it."

"I will, Lucy, but then I must depart."

"I know, Sam. I know."

For one moment, her green eyes took on the sad look of apprehending a world lost, and then the satirical look, much to Sam`s relief, returned.

Chapter 8

When he got home that night, his wife Mima had left him some cheese and bread and a mug with the last of the day`s milk, and had retired to bed. He quickly finished the little supper, and then, as quietly as possible and without taking a candle, he went upstairs, undressed and slipped into bed.

"Goodnight, Sam," she murmured in a sleepy voice.

"Goodnight, Mima. Didn`t mean to wake you up."

"I wasn`t sleeping. I had one eye open."

"Come here, then, and give me a hug."

She turned over towards him, and soon she was asleep in his arms. He lay awake for some time, reflecting on the blessings of a peaceful hearth and a good wife. He had stayed out later than he intended, but it was as far from her nature to reprimand him as it would be to scold her own children, or anyone else`s, for some minor misdemeanour. To express displeasure at other people, was, somehow, to hurt herself.

A gusty wind had blown up outside, and he heard it whistling around the eaves, and tugging at the boughs of the apple tree in the yard outside. To hear it thus, from inside, was to increase the sense of safety and comfort, and yet, in his still unsleeping thoughts, the sounds of the restless wind struck an uneasy chord. The world as a whole was not as good a place as it promised to be when he felt the warmth and sufficiency of Mima`s close embrace, and his meeting with Lucy Brindle had served to renew the sharp edged tooth which sometimes gnawed at his conscience.

When his father had been a governor at the workhouse in Salford, he had mixed, as a boy, with the paupers, the mad, the distracted, the ruined, those who had destroyed themselves and those who had been destroyed by circumstance, by drink, or sometimes by the malice of others, and his youthful desire to do something with his life to make the world a better place for such poor creatures, had been offset, as time and experience made their mark on him, by the sense that the world`s harsh machinery continued and would always continue to churn out victims, regardless of vice or virtue, regardless of deserving or otherwise, regardless of justice, love, religion.

That very thing, he had partly realised, was the very lesson that religion taught – submission to the uncertainty of fate, acceptance of misery, or of joy cut short, indifference to fortune, good or ill, in favour of the greater life to come. And yet what spirited young fellow with strong blood flowing in his veins can fully accept such a lesson without rebellion getting the better of virtuous passivity?

His own rebellion had been of the madcap kind which had taken him, aged eighteen, to South Shields to throw himself into the uncertain life of a rating on a merchant-man. It was the same rebellious nature which had made him jump ship in port at London, and make his way home, on foot, mile by mile, with scarcely a penny in his pocket, and risking, all the time, in every garrison town through which he passed, impressment to the armies and navies for the wars with Bonaparte. His own rebellion, too, had been of the kind which, in another kind of excess, had taken him, once, to a shadowy back alley in Manchester where he had all but debauched himself with Lucy Brindle.

"I will confess the whole thing to Mima, tomorrow," he said to himself. "I will tell her everything. I will trust in her gentleness, and her mercy, and her forgiveness."

So saying, or, at least, so thinking, Sam Bamford, still hearing the unappeased wind outside, but feeling now the calmness of his resolution, fell asleep at last in the warmth of his Mima`s arms.

31

Chapter 9

When Joseph Howarth, commonly known as Owd Scrat left his place beside the warm hearth of the tap-room of the Old Boar`s Head, it was past eleven o'clock. A wind had blown up, and he instinctively pulled the collar of his great-coat up around his neck. It wasn`t a cold wind – and anyway there was sufficient warmth emanating from the quantity of liquor he had within to offset any coldness in the night outside – but it was sharp enough to make his eyes water and his vision bleary.

It had been a good night. There was work set for two or three nights hence, and no-one could ever say it was easy work either, but tonight had been a night for enjoyment and self-indulgence, and accordingly, he had made the most of it. There was only one thing wanting, now, to turn a good night into an excellent night, but that one thing, he acknowledged ruefully, would have to wait until the next time he was in Manchester, where such a commodity was more readily available.

He had just turned into the narrow lane which led up to the Warren, and was approaching the stile which marked its first section, when there appeared before him a vision which so corresponded with the tendency of his own immediate thoughts that at first he thought it might be of diabolic origin and no real thing at all. It did not, however, disappear as he approached nor slip away into the shadows of the night; indeed, as if to prove beyond all doubt that it was corporeal in nature, the vision spoke, hailing him by his own name.

"You remember your Lucy, don`t you?" the vision added.

Well, in fact, Scrat did not remember his Lucy. Either because his brain was befuddled with drink, or because he had never met her before in the first place, he did not remember her at all, but he was not about to admit to this, especially since the suggestion that she was *his* Lucy argued a degree of intimacy that he found not without interest.

"Of course I remember you, Lucy. How could I forget you!"

The womanly form which he now saw before him at close quarters was, it seemed to Scrat, as unforgettable as, at least for present purposes, he might want it to be. Whether the bleariness of his eyes in the wind, or the benign effects of drink rendered undistinguishable to him the worn and grubby clothes, the coarsened skin, the premature lines and the livid bruise on her cheek, what in fact he saw, quite simply, was a descendant of Eve.

He produced a half-crown from his pocket and pressed it into her hand.

"For the love of God, then, Lucy, give me ease!"

He led her on, over the stile, towards a secluded spot of ground where, despite the recent rain, he proposed to himself that the transaction might be completed. She allowed herself to be drawn easily behind him, and Scrat thanked the good fortune that had thrown her in his way.

But then, having reached the spot, and just as he was about to slip down his breeches, she stepped back.

"What`s the matter, Lucy?" he said. "You`ve had my money, haven`t you? You`re not going to renege on the bargain now, are you?"

"I was hoping you`d lead me to a soft bed, not piece of hard turf! Is this the best I`m worth?"

"Course not," said Owd Scrat, now on his guard, wondering whether or not to cut and run, and let her make off with her ill-gotten half-crown.

"Well, then," she said, now stepping forward and reaching her hand into his breeches, where his manly pride, about to begin its abatement, was now persuaded otherwise.

She sucked in with her breath.

33

"You can have your half-crown back," she said, "but I need a comfortable bed to do proper justice to this."

"All right, then," said Scrat, his resolve gone. "And I'll give you another half-crown on top of that one, but you must be gone by morning, and by that I mean gone for good, and no dispute, is that understood?"

When Owd Scrat awoke in the morning, he remembered everything up to this point and very little beyond. He remembered taking Lucy to the house, and he remembered lighting a candle and taking her upstairs. After that he could remember nothing. Whether she had done justice to him, or he to her, was lost in the bottomless abyss of things forgotten.

But the main thing was that she was gone. He was glad of that. Owd Scrat made it a general rule not to have people in his house.

He went to the top of the stairs and listened from the landing. There was no sound. So far so good. He went down the stairs into the hallway with its dried out and worm-eaten wainscot. Still no sound. Good. He looked at the front door. The two main bolts were drawn, and the mortice turned, so that only the latch held the door shut. Good again. The filthy wench had let herself out. He breathed a sigh of relief, and turning from the door, closed his eyes and leaned back against it. What utter folly had persuaded him to let her come back to the house! He should have taken her there, down in the clearing, as was the nature of such a bargain, and whilst he was still keen for it, before the last hour`s drinking had caught up with him. If he`d had pleasure of her then, he would have remembered it, whereas now, for all he knew, it was two half-crowns as good as thrown into a cess-pit. Unless, of course – and here he squeezed his eyes tighter - she had fleeced him of more. If she was sufficiently clear-headed to let herself out and fasten the latch behind her, she was no doubt sufficiently clear-headed to go through his breeches and his coat to see what else she might carry off with her.

34

He made his way into the kitchen where his great-coat was hanging on the door. His pocket book was still there, and some loose change, all of which boded well. It was unlikely that she would have found the stash hidden in his mattress, or the stash hidden under the floorboards; if anything, she`d be the kind who just took what was at hand, and since his pocket book was there she must have gone off satisfied with her night`s earnings.

He began to feel easier.

It was only when he looked towards the cellar door, and saw that the padlock and chain, unfastened, were lying loose on the table close by, that gouts of sweat began to break out on his brow and a painful tingling to thrill at the roots of his hair.

If she`d been down there, he put it to himself, God alone knew what might be the outcome of it!

He tried to calm himself down and force remembrance into his mind. If he`d come home alone, he might well have slipped the key from round his neck, unfastened the padlock and descended to the first cellar to fetch up a bottle of brandy or a flagon of wine to provide a drop of something for a night-cap; but almost certainly, so drilled was he in the habit, drunk or sober, he would have fastened the chain and padlock up again, and put the key back round his neck. But here was the key still in the padlock, and here was the padlock and chain on the corner of the table. Had he been so befuddled with drink and lustful anticipation that he had opened up the cellar, in order to have something beside the bed, for afterwards, and then had forgotten to lock it again?

He knew not the answer.

The question was this: had she been down there, and if so, what had she seen?

For the fact was there were things in Owd Scrat`s cellar that had no business being there at all.

Chapter 10

When Sam Bamford awoke, the sun was smiling on a bright fresh morning, its beams dancing merrily around the edges of the shutters as if exhorting everyone within to be up and about, and all Sam Bamford`s gloomy thoughts had vanished like spectres of the night.

At the foot of the stairs, by the main door, his leather pack was waiting, and he remembered what he had forgotten last night, that it was `bearing home` day, the day when he took the wallet, full of the finished work back to the putter-out in Manchester, and to pick up his earnings and a wallet of fresh work. It had always been once a month when the work was steady and regular, but now it varied, being sometimes a month`s worth, sometimes as little as a week.

"I came upon an old acquaintance of ours last night," he said to Mima, as they broke their fast with milk and bread.

"Oh, and who was that?"

Sam said the name of Lucy Brindle and watched Mima`s face, as the clouds of thought resolved themselves into the clarity of memory.

"Poor Lucy," said Mima. "Was it not the story that she went to find her kinfolk in Leeds?"

"Such was the story," Sam replied. "But I fear the streets and taverns of Manchester are the closest thing she has to a home now."

"Is that what she told you?"

"I saw her there once, when I was working at the warehouse at Greengate."

"You never said."

"I didn`t think of it again, why should I?" said Sam, easing himself, not without some discomfort, past the awkward part of the story. "Not until I chanced to see her in the Boar`s Head last night."

"And what`s brought her back to Middleton?"

"She was looking for someone, some acquaintance or other. She was the worse for drink. I don`t know if she had a very clear sense of her own purpose."

"You must keep a look out for her, Sam," said Mima, beginning to clear away the plates. "Maybe we can perform some service to help her; Lord knows, that poor family had a hard time enough of it, through no fault of their own and there, but for the grace of God, go you or I, or any one of us."

"Indeed," Sam replied, recalling his own troubled thoughts of the previous evening, though hoping that Mima did not expect him to try over-zealously to seek Lucy Brindle out as an object for their charity.

Within quarter of an hour, Sam had set out on his way to Manchester. At home it was a day for Mima to clear out and tidy the loom-shop, and then go down into Middleton village to shop for groceries at the shambles.

The home of Sam Bamford and his wife, Mima, on Cheapside, in Middleton was arranged thus: there was one main room which was called the `house`; on the same floor was a loom-shop capable of containing four looms, and behind that a small kitchen and buttery bar. On the floors above were another small apartment and the bedchambers. When work was plentiful, Sam and Mima managed all four looms between them, though sometimes, depending on the vagaries of demand, which often went with the vagaries of war, one or more of the looms lay still. Close by the looms was a treddle whose purpose was to wind on bobbins as the looms required, and this task was performed variously by Mima, when the work was slack, by her aunt, who occupied an upstairs apartment in the household, and who complained incessantly that her rheumatic fingers made winding a very devil of a task, and by Simon, an orphan-lad of fifteen who had been taken out of the care of the parish as a child by another relative of Mima who had subsequently died.

It was also Simon`s job – as it had once been Sam`s to bring the milk from the milk-house on Hollin Lane first thing each day, and to fetch water, together with any other tasks and errands that were required and which suited a lad of fifteen better than sitting for any length of time at a treddle. The final member of the household was Bess, Mima`s younger sister, who was twelve, and who helped with the nursing of the children and with the care and upkeep of the house.

Chapter 11

Mima`s mother, when she was alive, had often said of Simon, the foundling child her cousin had rescued from the parish, that he was rather more like a girl than a boy. "You could dress him up in a bonnet and petticoats," she used to say, when he was five or six years old, "and he would look, for all the world, like a lass or a little porcelain doll."

The child had a delicate appearance, it was true, and a pallid complexion, though there was nothing delicate about his health or constitution. As he became older he grew slim and tall, with fair hair, naturally curving lashes, and striking blue eyes. In his nature, he was gentle and trusting, with a pleasant laughing temperament, but, exposed as he was to taunts and bullying, he had developed a defensive edge which sometimes made him brittle and abrasive.

"Tha looks like a reet queer mary-ellen, our Frank says," said one lad, at the milk-house, one morning, when he was fourteen. "He says he`d shag thi if he could find reet hole for it."

"I dare say God made me how he wanted me," said Simon, "and I thank him for not making me like thee, a troll with no neck and a donkey`s brain."

In the skirmish which followed, until it was broken up before any real harm could be done, Simon gave as good as he got, but after that he became wary and tended to take himself off alone and be company to himself, rather than mix in with the crowds.

One day, not long after he and Mima were married, Sam, out on a Sunday afternoon stroll in Middleton Woods, found Simon, almost hidden from sight, reclining on his elbow beneath a line of elder trees over-arching the river.

"Are you all right, chap?" he called. "Come, walk alongside me and we`ll enjoy a stroll together."

The young lad lifted himself from his secluded place and followed.

"I think he has a touch of melancholia about him," Sam said to Mima.

"Give him some of your books of poetry to read, Sam. That`d be good for him, I`m sure."

Sam gave him Lycidas and Il Penersoso, but though the lad seemed grateful, he showed no sign of having the application to make sense of them and draw the sustenance of their vivid meaning.

"What about the girls then?" said Sam, in jocular fashion, on another Sunday afternoon stroll he had persuaded Simon to accompany him on. "Aren`t there any you find yourself a little bit in love with?"

Sam was consulting his own reminiscences, for at the same age as Simon, he had been a little bit in love with almost every girl he came across. "What about Molly Brooks or Alice Gilbertson?"

"Molly has a very pretty bosom, which she takes great pains to display, and Alice has very white teeth, and such lips that you would want to kiss, just for the sake of kissing them, but I could never fancy myself being in love with any of them."

"I`ve done everything I can," Sam said to Mima. "I don`t know which way to turn next."

"Everything will work out," said Mima, putting her hand over his, "and God bless you for trying. But God has a plan for everything, and I`m sure he has a plan for our Simon, too."

Chapter 12

Lady Mary, eldest daughter of the last Baronet, Ralph Assheton, of Middleton Hall, and wife of Sir Harbord, Lord Suffield, had become an embittered lady. An bitter old lady, some people said, linking the words as if it were that potent combination of age and asperity alone that rendered her short-tempered, impatient, irascible, but it wasn't altogether so.

The tragic thing was that her brother Edward had died in his youth, tragic not merely because she loved him for himself, which she did, but because with him ended the family's male line. What might have been seen, after the mourning was done, as her good fortune - for as the eldest daughter, the estate was now to become her portion when her father died - had also been her misfortune, for she was convinced now that without a blood-line Assheton there to maintain its history and traditions, the hall and its grounds, pleasantly situated at the lower end of the peaceful township, close to the confluence of the River Irk and the Whit Brook, would fall into neglect and ruin, indeed were already doing so.

When the young Harbord had courted her, in London and in the beautiful family home at Gunton in Norfolk, all those years ago, when he had taken her to listen to the oratorios of Handel and Boyce and Scarlatti, and when they had visited Bath and Harrogate, amidst all that high-flown talk of love, had he been all the time looking beyond to the acquisition of Middleton?

Her younger sister, Eleanor, had married Sir Thomas Egerton of Radcliffe, and she saw her now only occasionally in London. It was true, also, that she herself had been happy enough to live away from Middleton in those early years, full of the distractions of married and family life.

There were people who said that Harbord – later Lord Suffield – had served Middleton well. Who but he had petitioned the House, in 1791, for a Royal Charter to hold a weekly market and annual fairs? Was it not Lord Suffield who, at his own expense, had the market house, and shambles built?

"Vulgar!" her mother, then still alive, had pronounced it all. It was too near the gardens. The cries of hucksters could be heard from dawn till dusk on market days and it attracted tinkers and mountebanks, ragamuffins and vagabonds. What about peace and tranquillity, were they no longer virtues to cherish?

"Madam," Harbord would reply, always in his most reasonable of tones, the one she had learned was his most dangerous and most determined, "I pay taxes on a great deal of land hereabouts, am I not to raise money by encouraging commerce? If I am ever to restore Middleton to its former glory, it must be paid for..."

"Try to see it from his point of view," she said - always the appeaser in those days – to her mother.

"He means to sell it," her mother, ever mistrustful, retorted. "You see if he doesn`t. He means to build up the value of the land and then sell it."

"He means to restore it," she insisted, though gradually, over the years, she had come to doubt it.

And over the years, too, as her husband and her two sons had occupied themselves with their business and their politics, discussing events in Paris, the independence of the Americas, the threats to the colonial trade, she had begun to long, in her middle years, with all the yearning of a young girl, for Middleton, the beautiful parkland and the hall, the rivers and the lake, the surrounding hills and woodland.

"Middleton Hall," she would repeat to herself, as if it were a soothing mantra. "Lovely Middleton Old Hall."

It was in the old plaster and framework style, dating back to the time of the first Sir Ralph Assheton who had served Richard III, and though there had been additions and accretions since, in different styles, it still had an aura of true antiquity; inside, too, with its panels, carvings, and beams of black oak, and the high ceilinged hall, hung round with matchlocks, swords, targets, and hunting weapons, intermingled with trophies of the battle-field and the chase, it spoke of centuries of tradition.

"Go there, if you wish," said Harbord, his reasonable tone influenced more and more, as time went on, towards irritation by his gout and his rheumatism. "Go there, if you wish."

And so she had, more than once.

But the house was becoming decrepit and the park untended and overgrown. She employed gardeners – that bit was easy. The requirements of the house were more difficult. The local builders and carpenters lacked the skill; those who had the skill required more than just a say-so, and no immediate answers came from Harbord, in Norfolk.

And then, from Norfolk, came the news that Harbord was dead. She did not attend his funeral. By the time she knew of it, the funeral was already set, and it was too far for her to travel. He would not have expected it.

Her sons were solicitous, but not passionate.

To them, Middleton meant little and it was no wonder. They had seldom been here, though of course William would now inherit the estate, and would have to drag himself away from his beloved cricket, and his parliamentary business, at least to come and take stock.

But here she was now, seventy years old and with little to look forward to. It was almost as if, like the hall itself, with the walls cracking and the plaster crumbling, she belonged in the past. Sitting at the window of the drawing room, on the first floor, with its view over the lake, and with the wooded slopes of Alkrington beyond, she reflected on how sad it was that all this, and all it represented, would one day be gone.

Another letter to William, she decided, was necessary, a letter reminding him of his new responsibilities and impressing on him a sense of the urgency which certain matters required. It was quite possible that, like his father, he would see the Middleton estate primarily as a source of revenue, but at least, if she got him to come here, she could make some attempt to use a mother`s influence.

Having resolved to go straight away to her escritoire to carry out this task, she was in fact still sitting at the window languidly taking in the view some forty minutes later when her maid Tessa entered the room and told her that Mrs Canky was waiting downstairs, if she would care to see her.

"Mrs Canky? Is she due today?"

"If it were up to me, she would not be due any day, ma`am."

"No, well it`s not up to you, is it, Tessa!" said Lady Mary, with some firmness. Tessa had been with her for fifteen years and was as much a companion as a lady`s maid, but there were times when she overstepped the mark.

"What do you think of Mrs Canky?" she asked Tessa, following the first occasion of Mrs Canky`s visiting the house.

"Very common, if you don`t mind me saying so, your ladyship," replied Tessa, who was sensitive, despite her own humble upbringings, on the subject of gentility. "And outrageously talkative. I can still feel her tongue buzzing in my head even now!"

Tessa was, Lady Suffield realised, a little jealous of Mrs Canky. Tessa had been trying to achieve her own modest level of gentility for so long that she had become a little sere and dry, like old parchment. Besides, Tessa was a Norfolk girl, and she had a thoroughgoing distrust of the Lancashire folk in whose midst she now found herself, and not least of their manner of speech.

"They speak in such an odd broken misbegotten fashion it`s a wonder any poor educated Christian soul can understand a word they say!"

But Lady Suffield had a sneaking liking for Mrs Canky. She had first called at the hall to deliver some little pieces of silk work that Lady Suffield had commissioned; it was only by chance that she had had any direct contact at all with the young woman on that occasion, but coming across her in the vestibule, waiting, somewhat ironically as it turned out, for Tessa, Lady Suffield had inspected the work herself and found it rather pretty.

"Thank you ma`am. I allus does my best to please, and if it`s reet then am glad."

The local tones and colours, of which Tessa so disapproved, were music to Lady Suffield`s ears. They recalled the magical years of her childhood, when, careless of rank, she and her brother and sister had slipped out of the park and had run headlong with the children from the forge and the mill along the river bank towards Rhodes, or across through Tonge to the White Moss. Her mother had disapproved, but her father, the last of the long line of Sir Ralphs, had blinked an eye, wanting them, as she heard him say, to be hearty and not spoilt by pride – at least until Edward had died, aged eleven. After that, her father had become withdrawn from the world and had paid little attention to his other children as they grew up.

A little later, of course, she might have married Ashton Lever from Alkrington Hall, who was high-spirited and eccentric, and with whom, as a seventeen-year-old, she had been madly in love, but her father, who regarded Ashton as a crackpot, had, rousing himself from his lethargy, put a stop to that.

To Lady Suffield now, fifty-odd years later, and with a tendency towards bitterness and impatience, Mrs Canky was a breath of fresh air.

Chapter 13

It was 'bearing home' day, and Sam Bamford had set out to walk the six miles to Manchester, taking the completed work – mainly romoll and pollicat handkerchiefs, and silk and cotton garments – back to the putter-out. On the way, he fell in with half a dozen other Middleton weavers on the same business, and they walked on together, in good spirits generally, though with the usual gripes. The main complaints were the high rents, with which the name of Harbord, Lord Suffield was usually associated, masters cutting payments, and the talk of mills and factories with steam powered looms which were springing up like mushrooms, some said, across the country.

"Progress they call it!"

"Lust after money and power, more like, it'll turn the masters into tyrants and the workmen into a multitude of slaves."

"We've already one at Middleton, at Ezekiel Barton's on Wood Street, and that's enough."

"I've heard it said that Ned Ludd is due a visit there, what do you say to that, lads!"

There was a chorus of laughter and agreement, though there was none who took the suggestion with any real seriousness. Despite the most pessimistic of predictions, and the perennial hardships, there were few who thought that the old ways would change entirely.

Reaching Long Mill Gate, the group split up to go to their respective destinations, Sam Bamford's being Messrs Samuel and James Broadbent of Cannon Street. Here he unpacked his wallet of the finished work, and waited for it to be checked, as it was by the genial old Mr Broadbent himself. "Very good, Sam," he muttered to himself as he progressed through the work, "very good, but no less than we've come to expect. Now

I've got a decent sized poke for you to carry home this time, not big, mind you, but decent enough, but it'll not be ready until this afternoon, so you'd better go down to the counting house and get what's due to you, and then come across the way with me, and have some dinner with us."

This kind of hospitality was not uncommon, the mistress having prepared a baked pudding or some broth with dumplings, though sometimes Sam went to the Hope and Anchor, by the old churchyard, where the other Middleton weavers would go for a lunch of cheese or cold meat and bread and ale, and then to the market on Mill Gate to buy a few treats, some tobacco for himself, some apples, and a posy of violets for Mima.

When he had picked up his wallet for home, he set off on the return journey, and again it was common for the Middleton lads to sidle along until they fell in together to make a group, partly for company, and partly – especially in winter when the darker nights were coming in – for protection as the road wasn't entirely free of foot-pads. In the hottest weather, some of the weavers would leave their poke at the Three Crowns in Cock Gates, to be brought on by the Middleton carrier, but Sam didn't like doing that for fear of stuff going missing, though as far as he knew nothing of that sort had ever happened. "Still," he would say, "if it's on my back, I know where it is!"

Usually, the group stopped at the White Lion in Blackley for a pipe and a thirst-quencher to set them up for the last leg of the journey, and after half an hour would set out up Hill Lane, the last climb before reaching home.

As he passed the Boar's Head, with the evening light now fading to a close and moth-like dusk, making the lighted tallows at the window all the more appealing, he was tempted to stop by, but remembering the previous evening, and also knowing that Mima would have something special waiting for his repast, he overcame the temptation, and was immediately glad that he'd done so.

47

Inside, he set down his poke in the loom-shop, and stretched his arms, glad at last to be rid of the weight, and then proceeded to the house. There, much to his consternation, sitting before the fire, wrapped in a blanket, and with Mima kneeling before her offering broth from a spoon, was Lucy Brindle.

Mima looked towards him with earnest and determined eyes, the eyes of someone who has made a moral decision and is going to stick by it, come what may.

"I found her by the shambles," she said, stirring the broth and then offering another mouthful. "She was shaking and shivering and quaking, I thought she was about to have a fit. Something`s happened to her, Sam."

Sam was tempted to say, "Drink! That`s what`s happened to her!" for he had seen such effects on those who have travelled far along the highways and by-ways of strong liquor, but when he`d seen her the previous evening he hadn`t thought she was as far gone as this.

"She hasn`t uttered a word," said Mima. "I hardly think she knows where she is."

Sam stepped forward into a direct line of vision. The girl seemed unaware of his presence, or, indeed, that she was the subject of the conversation. Shortly afterwards, another shaking fit began, and it was all Mima could do to hold her still in the chair. At last, after ten minutes, she quietened down, and her body went limp, as if in a swoon.

"I think she must be exhausted," said Mima. "We`ll put her in the little room on the second landing, and I`ll sit with her in case she wakes in the night. You`ll have to carry her, Sam, she`s beyond walking up stairs, I think."

With Mima`s help, Sam lifted her from the chair and began to carry her upstairs. She was light as a feather, but, close to, there was a pungent staleness to her clothes, and a reek of old liquor.

Once in the bed, she lay still, and Mima took off her shoes and her outer jacket, and then pulled a cover round her. Then, to Simon, who had led the way up the stairs with a candle, and was now standing in the doorway, "sit by her for a moment," she said, "whilst I see to Sam`s dinner and the house. I`ll be no more than twenty minutes."

Simon nodded.

"If she stirs, call me straight away."

He sat down at the chair by the bed, and Mima`s footsteps were heard going down the stairs.

Quarter of an hour later, when she returned, the room was still quiet.

"She opened her eyes once," said Simon, "but she seemed quite peaceful."

"Good lad," said Mima. "You can get off to bed now."

"Goodnight, then Mrs Bamford."

"Good night, Simon. God Bless!"

Chapter 14

After a night`s sleep in a clean bed, Lucy Brindle seemed, much to Mima Bamford`s relief, to have regained some of the mental composure which she had lacked the day before; after she had sipped some tea, an infusion of lime flowers, she was sufficiently alert to begin asking where she was and how she had got there.

"This is Sam Bamford`s house, and I`m Mima; you remember us from the old days, don`t you? I`m Sam`s wife, now. I found you in the market place, yesterday, and brought you here."

To this Lucy nodded, sometimes pausing, as if waiting for something to fall into place, but then nodding again as if it was all beginning to make a piece.

"Something must have shocked you, or frightened you. Do you remember?"

Lucy nodded her head slowly.

"Do you remember what it was?"

Lucy stared into the air for a few moments and then shook her head quickly. Seeing that her hand was beginning to tremble again, Mima quickly changed the subject.

"There`s a tub of hot soapy water down in the kitchen, Lucy. I`ll help you take these old clothes off, and when you`ve had a nice wash and a soak, I`ll let you have some of my own to put on, for I think we`re pretty much of a size."

Lucy was reluctant to part with her crimson velveteen jacket and skirt, and her feathered chapeau, which had evidently once been fancy, and which she regarded as so still, but on the understanding that they would be cleaned and kept for her, she at last agreed to undress and get into the tub.

"Give me your ring and your beads, Lucy, and we'll put them in a safe place."

For a moment, Lucy's face took on a defensive expression, but then, as if knowing that she could trust Mima, she took them off.

"They're very pretty," said Mima.

Lucy smiled. The ring and the beads were no more than cheap trinkets, but the rich green colour complimented her eyes, and she was evidently very proud of them.

"Let me do your hair for you," said Mima. "You've got lovely long hair when it's loose, but it's matted in places."

She was passive as Mima worked at the tangled knots, and later, when she was dried, and sitting in one of Mima's plain calico smocks, she allowed her to brush out the hair, so that it hung down over her shoulders onto her back and her breast.

"I awoke in the night," said Lucy, "and I was frightened, but then I thought I saw an angel sitting beside my bed and I knew I was safe."

"Perhaps it was an angel," said Mima.

Later, when they were at table and Simon came in to join them, she noticed Lucy staring at him, and remembering what Simon had said about her opening her eyes, Mima smiled. There's your angel for you, Lucy, she said to herself.

"What are we going to do with her, though?" asked Sam, when, at the end of the day, they had some time together alone.

"She's been sent to us so that we may do her some good. You says she's a fallen woman, but then, according to the scripture, so was Mary Magdalene and she waited on our lord in his hour of need on the cross."

"The scripture's all very well," said Sam, "but we have practical things to consider, and though we may keep her a while, there can be no permanent place for her in our household, you know that as well as I."

"With a little time and kindness, though, Sam, maybe she will see that there is a better and more godly way. And then, perhaps, we can find her a place, where she may live a useful and respectable life, and find contentment."

Sam nodded assent. In Mima`s goodness, there was sometimes that which was inconvenient, stubborn, even, but he deferred to it; her goodness it was, after all, which was his own touchstone of faith and certainty.

Chapter 15

Mrs Canky was entertaining Lady Suffield with an account of the various supernatural beings - boggarts, fyerin-folk, fairies, clap-cans, witches and other spirits – who lurked about the shadowy corners and melancholy places of the town, and in the neighbouring fields and lanes, and who, during the appointed hours of neet-gloom, came forth to wander where they would.

Mrs Canky did not offer her account in any way that was susceptible to doubt or enquiry. If anyone were to suggest – as some did from time to time – that she was speaking nonsense, she would give them a certain look, the same look she would give a man walking along a road towards a deep hole and turning his head back to deny the existence of any such hole, and would continue. Mrs Canky believed in the existence of spirits as much as she believed in the reality of her own flesh, and there was, let it be said, nothing more real than that.

Lady Suffield was well aware from the discourses of her late husband that the age of superstition was dead, and that it had been replaced by an age of reason. You should picture the world, he told her, trying to formulate an analogy which was within the intellectual grasp of one of the weaker sex, as a rather exquisitely made silver watch or clock. The creator has fashioned each delicate spring, each interlocking cog, each finely poised lever so that once set in motion the mechanism works perfectly and without further intervention. This clockwork, my dear, is analogous to nature and the scientific laws God has written into nature; man`s duty is to unlock those laws and put them to the service of mankind, for the greater glory of God.

Lady Suffield, however, did not see it as her business, when in conversation with Mrs Canky, to correct the misguided young woman and point out the errors in her thinking. She had no desire that her young, and as Tessa saw her, rather common and vulgar acquaintance should be brought to understand that the world, and all within it, operated according to exactly the same principles as a gentleman`s fob-watch.

Quite the opposite.

It was an anodyne to Lady Suffield`s bitterness and an antidote to her boredom, to encourage Mrs Canky in her picturesque and ghoulish imaginings.

"So you say, Mrs Canky, that Owler Bridge is a place much to be dreaded?"

"Much to be dreaded indeed, ladyship."

Lady Suffield knew Owler Bridge well; it was less than quarter of a mile from the point where the Whit Brook met the Irk, carrying the footpath across to Hilton Fold, and not fifteen minutes` walk from the hall.

"T` field twixt Back-o`th`-Brow and Owler Bridge is thronging wi` spirits, mam, and there`s fairees gambolling from dusk to dawn on the bridge and on the banks each side."

"And you`ve seen this yourself?"

"That I `ave, mam, as true as I sit `ere, an` many another, too."

"But they pose no harm, do they, surely?"

"Not if you remember to say the words of a psalm, or just hum the tune of a hymn, as you pass, if you must pass, but best not to. They say a foul murder was done thereabouts, in the old days, and where a murder`s been done, the owd lad and his minions have free range, at least that`s how I understand it."

"Fascinating," said Lady Suffield. "And yet the picture of fairies gambolling is not altogether a frightening one, rather quite the opposite."

"So you might say, mam, and so a man might think, and many has, but I`d not let my husband stray down that way of a neet, not if I could help it, and your ladyship'll forgive me if I don't say why!"

Here, Mrs Canky let out a small ripple of self-indulgent laughter. "Indeed," said Lady Mary, glad that Tessa had excused herself from the meeting.

"Stanicliffe Hall, up near Hopwood, is another place," Mrs Canky went on, "which has very bad demons. The fyerin-folk come there sometimes in the form of a calf, sometimes in the form of a black dog, trotting along the corridor, behind you or towards you, and that's to do with old Blomly, who'd become so vicious through the blood he'd spilled and seen spilled in the civil wars that he had the habit of killing who he pleased by his own hand. And even after the vicar had been there, with his bell and his book and his candle, sounds could still be heard as if persons were holding a conversation in whispers, doleful cries, and crashes, as if every piece of crockery in the house was being broken, and yet, in the morning, everything would be found in its proper place. And if you don't believe me, you don't need to, because there's others, many and enough to crowd a session room with judge and jury who'd tell you exactly the same thing."

"I don't disbelieve you, Mrs Canky," said Lady Suffield, though before she had time to substantiate this, or to delve further into Mrs Canky's knowledge, there was a knock on the door, and Thomas, the footman, announced the arrival at the house of Mr Gregge Hopwood and his companion, Lord Byron.

"Show them into the drawing room," said Lady Suffield, somewhat wearily, for it was many years since the courtesies of polite society had held any charm. "Have Tessa bring up some tea."

"Very good, your ladyship."

"I'm afraid we must break off, Mrs Canky. Thomas will pay you for the work as you go out, and there are some other small patterns I should like you to follow."

"Thank you, ma'am. Am to come again then?"

"Yes. As soon as the work is done. Or before if you wish to show me what progress you`ve made. Come next Tuesday."

"Very good, mam."

On the stair, she passed Lady Suffield`s visitors. Squire Hopwood she knew well enough, but the other was a stranger. When she reached the foot of the stairs, she turned, and saw that the stranger had stopped and had turned also to look directly at her, so that she felt his eyes piercing her own.

"Who?" said Canky when she told him of her afternoon`s visit to the hall.

"Lord Brian, I think, or summat of the sort."

"Must be him I saw the squire with by the churchyard the other day."

"Such eyes he had," said Mrs Canky. "When he looked at me I come over all of a shiver. He had eyes just like th`owd lad himself."

Chapter 16

Ezekiel Barton was not of genteel stock, but he was welcomed in the houses of the local gentry as a man of enterprise and a man of ideas. The son of a hand-loom weaver, he had heard his father complain many times of how much time was wasted by those in the cottage trade – I`m walking here for this and there for that, I spend more time walking about than I do at the loom. For the bearing home days he reserved his sharpest tirades. Not for him the fellowship of other weavers, as they fell into step together on the pleasant walk to Manchester; not for him the leisurely stroll around the penny market, looking for nick-knacks and gewgaws to take home for his wife and weans. A day gone by, and a day wasted, he would say, disgruntled, when he reached home.

He managed to save enough, however, through his labour, to send his son Ezekiel to school in Manchester, and he was glad that the rest of his children were girls. `I hope it`ll do him some good,` he would say, `but I`ll tell you this, I couldn`t afford to put two sons through school!` Ezekiel was quick to learn reading and writing, but he wasn`t a brilliant scholar when it came to the classics, and the effort of painstakingly translating epic poetry in Greek and Latin took away, for him, much of the vaunted romance of the tales. He developed a curious and inquisitive mind, however, and one of his school fellows being the son of Samuel Greg of Styal, Ezekiel found himself being taken to visit the new mill at Quarry Bank, near Wilmslow, and that fired his imagination much more than the glories of Homer and Virgil.

At the age of twenty five, now a competent weaver himself, and married with a young son, he announced to his father that he was going to the bank to see about raising money to construct a factory.

"Th`art mad," said his father. "What ar`t going to do, wear thy best apron t`impress `em?"

"I`ll show `em this," said Ezekiel, producing a roll of drawings, which outlined the plan of a factory on three floors, set out with machinery, storage sheds, offices and a warehouse.

"And what`s this?" said his father, impressed, in spite of himself.

"That`s where the steam engine goes. And it's the steam engine that drives the looms."

"They`ll never go for it," said his father, so habituated in his belief that things just went on and didn`t get better, that he thought everyone else had that belief too.

"Look, dad, if you take all your complaints about what`s wrong with the trade, what with time wasted, and how slow it is, and how spread out, and if you take those complaints and put them in a pot and melt them down, this is what you`d come up with, like pure metal coming out of rough ore."

"Well, good luck to you, son. I just hope you don`t end up ruining yourself. Or ruining me, for that matter!"

But the old man was right about the bankers. They were used to dealing with a certain type of investor, and Ezekiel Barton didn`t fit the pattern. Undaunted, the young man had the idea of going to see the Squire at Middleton Hall, Sir Harbord, Lord Suffield, who had been sufficiently enterprising himself to set up a market, turning an otherwise sleepy village into a town.

Before the meeting had finished, Lord Suffield had already designated a plot of land, at the bottom of Wood Street, opposite the forge, which could be leased for the venture. He shook the young man`s hand, vigorously, and Ezekiel Barton felt a curious sense that in Lord Suffield he had made a friend, just as, at subsequent meetings, in the presence of Lady

Suffield, and her mother, Lady Assheton, he felt an equally curious sense that he had made not one, but two, inveterate enemies.

It was Lord Suffield's banker who next looked at the plans which Ezekiel Barton unfolded on the table. 'You bring the men and the machines into one place,` he argued, `under one roof. The men operating machines need not be so skilled as a hand-loom weaver, so long as their work is properly overseen. The operatives are paid less, but it still creates more work for more men than is the case now. And more prosperity, since even the lowly paid man, if he has money in his hand, will buy meat for his table and clothes for his back and coal for his fire. The capacity and speed of production will draw customers. An order placed in Manchester may take a month, two months to complete; an order in Middleton will take a week.`

He stopped there, knowing the point had been made.

Two months later, the first course of brickwork was laid.

Twelve months later, the factory was producing its first rolls of cloth.

And since then, Ezekiel Barton had become, in a quiet way, a familiar guest at the occasional parties of the surrounding gentry. His wife Melissa was the third daughter of an old Heywood family whose antiquity being much at odds with their wealth had no proper business having three daughters at all; but Melissa, being not only the prettiest of the three, but the most gentle, and most sweet-tempered, was accepted too by the local gentry, albeit with a little condescension, as one of their own.

Barton himself did not court the gentry for his own vainglorious ends. He was a chapel Methodist and his own manner of living was consistent with frugality and common-sense Christianity. But he liked to think that his wife, and his daughters, now twelve, eight, and six had a place of esteem in Middleton's society, and that his son, David would one day profit from the contacts it brought; and though he prayed, earnestly each night to be redeemed from the sin of vanity, no man, in reality, unless he is a saint, refuses to take some pleasure in the sense that his worth is recognised, and his achievements applauded.

Chapter 17

Oliver Canky wanted a son. It was, he supposed, a natural enough thing for a man to want, and he had every reason to believe that he was eminently capable of siring one. If the Good Lord had planted urges in man of precisely the kind that would ensure such an outcome, then he had surely planted enough of them in Canky to make the business safe.

The first Mrs Canky, having discovered on their wedding night such a shock at what was expected of her, and such a reluctance afterwards to repeat it, that it was only duty that made her succumb, as she did, at Canky`s insistence, twice a week, to the ritual of having her legs parted so that Canky could do what was needful.

But it was to no avail.

Canky blamed her, and told her that it must be her frostiness that was putting a curse on it. It certainly couldn`t be his fault. He had enough mettle, and more than enough, so much so that he was sometimes forced to disburse himself of a half-crown, in the less frequented streets and back corners of Manchester, to rid himself of the superflux thereof.

When he married his second wife, Jenny, and having, as it were, sampled the goods before he purchased, he was fairly confident that the pattern of his first marriage would not be repeated. Not only did he conjecture that soon there would be a little Canky or two to jog along at his heels, but he also promised himself some hearty sport at their making. In this latter respect, he was not disappointed, for, except when the shrewish fit persisted, which was not often, Jenny Canky had as lusty an appetite that way as any man could wish for in a wife. And yet, after five years of marriage, the parish register had not been troubled yet to record the christening of the first of the next generation bearing the name of Canky.

Jenny Canky was not without her own suppositions about the possible causes of her failure to conceive. More than once, she had heard old Mrs Henson, who was an aunt of the first Mrs Canky, muttering incomprehensible mumblings as she passed by the house, and she didn`t doubt that these mutterings were in the nature of a curse. Twice, when Canky himself had fallen asleep, bathed in the sweat of his own effort, she had opened the shutters to let in a little air, and had seen a black cat silhouetted against a full moon over the crest of the Warren, and that, she was convinced, was an omen. And there were others. "Every time I drain my tea," she said, "my heart`s in my mouth to see which way the leaves lie, and I seldom see anything to make me think there isn`t some fyerin business about it, and as I have nothing of conscience to reproach myself with, it`s my opinion that you might look no further than Lily Henson to find out what`s amiss."

Canky was not a man of superstition but almost against his own persuasion he found himself watching Lily Henson whenever he saw her. Once, sidling up behind her, he leaned towards her and said, "you keep yourself out of my business, Lily Henson, or you`ll be the worse for it," but she only turned to him with a benign and toothless smile. The truth was that Lily Henson had lost the best part of her wits long ago, and that she muttered and mumbled everywhere she went.

For this lapse, Canky reproached himself. He was a man of reason and science, for what was Canky`s trade, properly understood, but a matter of facilitating the onward progress of science?

A ragged old woman in the market place, who called herself a gypsy and told fortunes for a farthing, had once told Jenny Canky that her fate was to lie with the devil and bear him a child, and when she married Canky she was only half joking when she said to her friends that the first part of the prophecy had already come true. But to do her justice, Jen Canky herself was not averse to the approach of science. When Canky suggested that she might set herself on hands and knees, offering herself naturally, in the manner of beasts, she had been happy to comply, though more than once, Canky himself becoming disconnected at the crucial moment, the experiment had failed.

"You shouldn`t wriggle so much," he said, afterwards.

"You didn`t object to me wriggling when I was doing the wriggling!" she protested. "Not if I know anything about it."

She had agreed to stand on her head, after coition, to allow the law of gravity to lend its assistance to the good work which Canky had just done; she sat atop of Canky; she lay sideways on to him; she lay under him with her knees crooked over his shoulders, but none of these scientific methods had yet succeeded in getting Mrs Canky with child.

Canky sometimes wondered if Jenny didn`t have simples and preparations to avoid what they both professed to want.

Once, in a deeply persisting shrewish fit, she had declared, "why should I want to have your brats anyway Canky, why should I, when there`s that many as die when they`re about it, and others who grow fat as pigs after it, and others who end up thin as rakes, and allus sickening for something until they die, all for giving nothing but relief to the likes of you, Oliver Canky."

Sometimes, when she thought he was asleep, he watched her to make sure she wasn`t administering some antidote from her recipe book, some mixture of herbs, something compounded to an ointment, some draught mixed in with small beer.

But there was nothing.

"I`ll just have to try harder," he said, as if reproaching himself for neglect, one night in the Old Boar`s Head. He took a thoughtful sip of his mulled ale, and a half-smile might have been seen to play, momentarily, across his lip. "There`s only one thing for it, I`ll just have to redouble my efforts."

Chapter 18

Joshua Dyson, of the forge on Wood Street, opposite Ezekiel Barton`s new factory, was a man of few words. In the main few words were quite sufficient for his purposes, for the forge was a noisy place, what with the constant din of hammer on anvil and the roar of the bellows driven flame, and besides this, it was a hot, sweaty, dirty, laborious place where the art of conversation did not thrive. The business transactions of the trade required perhaps less than two dozen words in total, including a salutation and a valediction, together with a very rudimentary knowledge of figures, and so here again no special eloquence was demanded. When he went from the forge to the house at the end of the day, tired and ready for his modest evening fare and his pipe and his tankard of ale, he preferred to sit quietly before the hearth thinking his own thoughts, and in this, he was perfectly at one with his wife, Martha, so that if, between the hours of six and nine, fewer than a half dozen sentences were exchanged between them, it in no way indicated any disharmony in their domestic relations. When, at bed-time, Martha said her prayers aloud, she spoke for both of them.

There had always been a Dyson at the forge, back at least to Joshua`s great-grandfather, and like certain types of horse, bred specially for a certain type of job, the Dyson men, with their broad backs and stout necks, their powerful arms and bulging fists, their legs proportionately short, but therefore all the better for taking a firm and unshifting stance on the ground, seemed perfectly suited to the trade of blacksmith.

It was all the more strange, therefore, that Joshua and Martha`s first son should be such a slight and sketchy piece of work, and so sickly that it was thought for some time that this strangeness was not something that would need to be

64

pondered for long. By whatever narrow margin it was, however, the child survived, and it was only when he began to grow that certain imperfections and incongruities of physique and physiognomy, barely noticeable in the tiny infant were becoming more pronounced by the day.

People had different explanations for why this was so. Some argued that there must be a physical reason, such as, for example, the inhalation of some noxious vapour or other from the forge by Martha Dyson at the time when she conceived; others suggested a moral reason: that the child`s deformity must be the direct action of God for some sinful act or general state of sinfulness requiring punishment; others again put the case that some supernatural work was afoot, practised by a person or persons unknown, in the town, who had some grudge to bear or malice to exercise. It was generally agreed, however, that, whatever its cause, something had gone badly wrong in Martha Dyson`s womb, and that this was the result.

For a man such as Joshua Dyson, it was supposed, this must be a matter for disappointment and bitterness. In fact, nothing could be further from the truth. Whether, at some point during the uncertain time when he and his wife were measuring, day by day, the child`s afflictions, he had looked into some deep part of himself for an answer, no-one would ever know, but what was apparent, to all who witnessed it, was that, as the months and years passed by, no child, not the prettiest, not the cleverest, not the greatest adornment to his parents` hopes, could have been more loved, or could have given more glad-eyed joy to his doting father than did the poor little crippled boy, Daniel Dyson.

As he grew to the age when the little fellows of his own age were dashing wildly about in the meadows, climbing trees, and running after horses and dogs and sheep and rabbits, whatever moved, Daniel could walk no more than a dozen paces before the effort of so doing became a cause of pain. But his father carried him on his shoulder to Middleton Woods, and sat him down beside the river, or on a hillside, and together they would watch the world of nature going on around them. The child was thick of speech and many people took this to be a sign that he was slow of wit, but Joshua knew that this not so. Quite the opposite. The child's observations, for anyone who took the trouble and patience to understand them, were lively and astute, and he understood much more of other people than they understood of him.

One day, a Sunday afternoon, Joshua Dyson had taken Daniel to the bridge over the river, just inside Middleton Woods, and was holding onto him, sitting on the parapet, so that he could see the swift current flowing past underneath.

"If you were to let go of me now, dad," the child said, "you`d rid yourself of a great deal of trouble, that you would!"

"I would no more let go my hold on you, Daniel, than I would let go my hold on my own life, on my own eternal soul."

"I know, dad," said the child, feeling the grip of those strong arms tightening around him. "If it were your strength alone, then I know I would need fear nothing."

"Don`t cry dad," said the child, a few moments later. "It breaks my heart to hear you cry so. When I lie in my grave, I shall be at peace, and I know that when I awaken from that sleep I will be whole and perfect in the eyes of my redeemer."

"You`re perfect now," cried Joshua Dyson, from the depth of his agony. "You`re perfect now!"

This scene had taken place as recently as April, when the first fine tracery of green was weaving its way through the woodland trees, and when white and pink blossoms were beginning to unfold their fragile petals. A week later, the child was taken with a fever which gradually sapped away what little strength he had. Now, as the dawn broke over a silent forge, it brought with it the day of Daniel Dyson`s funeral.

"Come, Joshua," said his wife, trying to raise him from the chair next to the coffin where he had been sitting awake all night. "Let them do what they have to do."

"No," said Joshua, "I`ll not let any man`s eyes but mine be the last to see him in this world."

The undertaker`s men were sent from the room, and after a further five minutes of the deepest silence, a low scraping noise was heard, and then, slowly, one by one, the tapping in of the nails.

An hour later, the coffin stood on the wooden battens above the clean-cut shadowy hole which Oliver Canky had prepared the previous day, and the rector was reciting, in a dull monotone, the familiar litany of the burial service. This done, the battens were removed, and Canky and the three undertaker`s men, taking the strain of the ropes, lowered the coffin to its resting place beneath. Then, the rector and the undertaker`s men left the scene until, at last, just Joshua Dyson and Oliver Canky remained.

The blacksmith was kneeling at the side of the grave, peering down, as if he might yet take it into his mind to lift the coffin back single-handedly [which, Canky reflected, he most probably had the strength to do] or to throw himself into the hole, and let the earth be piled up on top of him as he lay there.

Oliver Canky, mindful of the piety of the scene, waited patiently. He watched as the great shoulders heaved, and listened as a stifled moan broke from the blacksmith`s throat. He waited again, until the heaving of the shoulders ceased, and then he kneeled down beside him, and put his hand on his back.

"Take comfort, man," he said. "Who could wish his body in a more peaceful resting place than this, or his soul in a better or more heavenly place than the one where it surely is already?"

"You`re right," said the smith, now in a calmer state.

"We mourn for ourselves, not for them. It`s not that we would keep them here, in this vale of tears, but that we must stay here without them."

At last, the blacksmith stood to his full height.

"Will you fill it in immediately?" he said, eyeing the pile of loam to one side of the grave.

"That`s why I`ve stayed behind," said Canky.

"He will be safe, won`t he?"

"You can be sure of that."

"It`s just that I`ve heard…" here the big man`s voice began to quiver and break at the thought of what he was saying.

"You need have no fear on that account," Canky reassured him. "A watch is always kept. I arrange it myself. There`s none of those goings on in this churchyard, of that I give you my solemn word."

"Thank you," said the blacksmith, and at last, much to Canky`s relief, he began to make his way back to the brow of the hill, where his wife was waiting by the lane.

Chapter 19

A midst the many rays of good fortune which shone into Ezekiel Barton`s life, there was one shadow, and that shadow obscured the place where his affections and hopes were most tenderly concerned, the place occupied by his son, David.

If Ezekiel himself had enjoyed advantages provided by a careful father, David had the same and more, for by the time the boy was growing up his father was already becoming a wealthy man. In gazing into his own fond crystal ball, Ezekiel saw his son going on to Cambridge, and thence to a career in one of the professions, in law, or commerce, or banking. The sad truth was, however, that as soon as David went away to school he began to apply himself steadily to the process of becoming a disappointment.

It wasn`t that he was a duffer, his masters said, but that he had no interest in learning and had a tendency to scoff and become insolent when challenged. His mother, who adored him, said that she believed it stemmed from his being homesick. In his private thoughts, Ezekiel Barton wondered if it wasn`t more the case that the boy had been over-indulged, especially by his mother, and led into selfish habits of thought as a child.

The process of talking to the boy and making him see sense, and hoping that a corner had been turned, went on for some years, but by the time he was sixteen it was fairly clear to Ezekiel Barton, looking back on it, that the route travelled by the boy had been almost without deviation. When, during the following Michaelmas term, there was an incident with one of the school servants, a girl of the same age, it was agreed that it was in the best interests of all concerned if the boy were removed.

At home, the boy sulked and complained, blaming everyone else for his misfortunes and fall from grace. His mother blamed Ezekiel for being so weak as to allow a mere serving-girl to be the means by which their son was cut off from his prospects. Ezekiel wrung his hands, and wondered what was to be done with the boy.

Eventually, a minor position as a clerk was found for him at the factory, on the understanding that if he proved himself to be competent, he would be kept on and given an allowance, and with the incentive that if he proved himself to be excellent, he would be advanced, within the family business, to positions of greater seniority.

It was not demanding work and a degree of competence just sufficient to meet the standard required by his father was, in due course, achieved. As he said to himself, with a wryness of humour for which he prided himself, he was not yet ready for excellence.

This had been the situation now for four, nearly five years, and in the meantime, with the assistance of his allowance, and, when needed, with additional funds which could easily be cajoled from his mother, he had developed himself in other directions.

He had acquired the tastes and mannerisms – if not the manners – of a gentleman. He was very particular in his dress, took pains to make himself a decent horseman, and had learned how to drink, play cards, and throw dice, skills which had been woefully neglected in his formal education.

He was not unhandsome, retaining, at the age of twenty-one, a boyishness of face which, though it had lost some of the youthful charm which his mother had always found endearing, and did so still, was still capable of expressing petulance when he did not get his way, smug self-satisfaction when he did, and somewhere in between, a kind of satirical arrogance towards anyone or anything he came across which he deemed to be beneath him.

To his father, as he begrudgingly acknowledged, he owed the social connections which made it possible for him to ride out, both for the hunt and the chase, with the local gentry, the Gregges of Hopwood, the Starkeys of Tonge, and so on, but he did not aspire to be so gentrified himself as to exclude others, of lesser rank, amongst the men - amongst the women too for that matter - which whom he chose to spend his idle hours.

He was as comfortable in the tap-rooms of the Boar`s Head, the Church Tavern, and the Assheton Arms as he was in the drawing rooms of Hopwood Hall, or Middleton Hall, or Alkrington Hall. And apart from his father, who grieved constantly but mainly in silence over his son`s profligate ways, and apart from a few others who laughed behind his back, he was generally thought to be a good sport, a jocular companion, and a man who more than paid his way – in short, a capital fellow.

Chapter 20

There was, amongst those who helped him to carry it out, a natural debate about the conditions most suitable to the successful execution of Canky`s trade. A moonlit night was, for obvious reasons, generally regarded as bad. And a star-lit night, even without the moon, was just as bad, if not worse. There was agreement about that. Some of his comrades favoured rain for the main reason that a good steady downpour, or a day-long misty drizzle, tended to keep other folk indoors, though others complained that the pathway winding round the Warren became sometimes so clogged with mud that they could hardly put one foot in front of another without slipping and sliding and being in danger of doing themselves a serious mischief in the near pitch blackness of that alley at the dead of night. It was only a short way to the river, however, and once you were on the river, the rain made no difference, unless you counted the fact that the rain tended to make things miserable, but for those who were engaged in Canky`s trade, considerations of misery or joy were not paramount.

Winter, despite the cold, was agreed on as better than summer. In winter, the margins of darkness were greater, and pleasant summer evenings often brought other sport to the banks of the river. Like all trades, however, Canky`s trade had to make a profit, had to balance supply and demand, and had to meet deadlines, and so seasonal variations, and the advantages and disadvantages they brought, simply had to be dealt with.

Canky himself, as the chief agent, and moreover, as the sexton, could do a great deal to make things easier by his careful preparatory work. Canky knew how, by putting in a temporary false ceiling to a newly inhabited grave, it could be made to appear that the same grave had been filled when in fact it hadn`t. Canky also knew that the best time to remove the nails or screws from the lid of a coffin was in the first ten minutes or so after the mourners had departed. By such shifts as these, the midnight business was made all the easier.

Sometimes, also, it was possible to remove a body from its casket, and transpose it temporarily to another newly dug grave nearby, awaiting its proper occupant on the next day or the day after that. Then the original grave would be back-filled on an empty coffin, and no-one any the wiser. It was risky, of course, for such a discovery, should it be made, would brook no explanation, and for this reason, Canky used it sparingly, and then only towards the end of the day when darkness was already falling, so that the temporary accommodation was only required briefly.

All this, of course, gave Canky the opportunity to remove necklaces, wedding rings, silver and gold lockets and other precious things which loving wives and husbands, parents and children had, in grief, been loath to remove, and hoping, perhaps that the love which they betokened when purchased would outlive the tomb, but this his comrades had to accept. They knew that he put some things back into the common pot, they knew that he didn`t put all things back into the common pot. This, having no choice in the matter, they accepted as reasonable.

But Canky had other arts, too, and these were sometimes necessary. Word of the resurrection men having spread, and the practice thus being a common fear, some families set watch over their newly laid graves, sometimes for as much as a week, and this was why Canky had offered, a humble and pious addition to his usual duties, to keep a watch over the graveyard.

But to those who kept a watchful eye, Canky knew that his device of making a grave appear to be back-filled when it wasn`t, was a potentially dangerous ruse. There were some occasions when a body ready for the trade had to be retrieved, not from under a false grave ceiling, but from under six feet of heavy loam.

A body was still good, Canky knew, for the purpose which the trade served, for as much as a week – longer in winter – after it had been interred. It was a leeway welcomed by the trade, though it did not make its business more pleasant.

But Canky, going about his normal sexton's business, also knew how to leave a pot hole, just big enough for a man to stand in, at the head of a grave, and how to break through the wood of a coffin, and attach ropes so that the coffin's tenant could be drawn out, and upwards, through the pot hole, without further ado, and the ground made good in minutes.

On the day of Daniel Dyson's funeral, as night drew on, it brought with it a steady wind, not loud or violent but enough to lift the boughs of trees, and disturb their tops with its murmuring, and to move the big covering clouds quickly across the sky. It was a good night for the trade. The only danger was that sudden breaks in the cloud might uncover the glimmering and tell-tale moonlight, but Canky knew that by midnight, when the best part of their work was still to do, the moon would have followed its trajectory far enough eastwards to be no longer a danger.

By the time his comrades joined him, he had already removed the pitifully thin corpse, and had wrapped it in sacking, and hidden it under a nearby hedge. Working quickly, he then began to heap the earth back into the hole. Were he to be discovered at this stage, it would be his downfall, he knew. But he trusted himself not to be discovered. For one thing, he worked in darkness, and for another he knew that anyone approaching – apart from his own men, of course – would approach with a lantern, for there were few, even amongst the most stout of heart who would cross a graveyard at night without one. If a lantern appeared, he would be off as nimbly as a cat, and within ten minutes would be in bed besides Mrs

Canky, his mind on other business, and leaving others to bring the news of the crime to him.

At last, the grave now nicely made, and the small wreath which had been on the coffin placed neatly on the mound, he heard footsteps approaching.

"How do, lads."

"How do," said Ned Small, echoed by Sam Forcher, and again by Bill Nimmy.

"All reet?"

"All reet."

"Where`s Scrat?"

"Said he`d meet us here."

"How come?"

"Have to ask him thissen. Been like cat on coals all day. Summat about an hoor he`s been watchin out for, I could make neither rhyme nor reason of it."

"Damn him!" said Canky. "He should keep his hooring in its proper place."

"Hush," said Bill Nimmy. "There`s some lad draws near. It`ll be him. Leastways, I hope it`ll be him."

All four men listened. The footsteps on the sward grew louder, and a moment later, Scrat emerged from the darkness.

"Where`ve you been?" said Ned Small.

"Hush!" said Canky, sharply. "Now we`re all here, we`ve work to do, so let`s get started."

"Have you got him out? Is he ready?"

"Ready as a bridegroom," said Canky, leading them to the place by the hedge where the mortal remains of Daniel Dyson lay, awaiting one last and unlooked for journey, wrapped up in sacking. "Light as a feather, too. It`s easy work for you lads tonight."

"Hark!" said Bill Nimmy, as they were lifting the burden.

"What is it, Bill?" said Ned. Bill Nimmy was generally credited with having the sharpest hearing.

"A horse," said Bill. "I can hear a horse, snorting."

"Where?"

"From up there, beside the church."

It was at that precise moment that through a sudden cleft in the cloud passing overhead, a shaft of moonlight revealed, in silhouette, the outline of horseman managing his restive steed, on the flat level beside the church.

Ned Small tried to speak, but could not, his power of speech locked by some force over which he had no power.

Bill Nimmy tried to scream, but could not do so, his powers similarly and utterly nullified.

"It`s the horseman of the apocalips!" said Scrat.

"It`s no such thing!" said Canky. "We can see him but he can`t see us, unless you draw him here with your prattling. Now, get started on your way, and let me sort with yonder horseman of the apocalips."

They obeyed his command, glad to be going in a different direction, and Canky made his own way up towards the church square.

"You`re out late, sirs," he said, for he found, on his approach that there was not one horseman but two.

"You`re out late yourself."

"Squire Hopwood," said Canky, "forgive me, I didn`t see who it was till now, and your lordship, I believe," he added, bowing.

The second horseman, Lord Byron, made a gesture of acknowledgment, but his horse turned away, and the rider had to bring him back in a circle.

He may have the devil`s eyes, said Canky to himself, remembering what Jen had said of him, but he`s no horseman, if I`m any judge.

"What do you do out this late, sexton?" asked the nobleman.

"I keep a watch, your lordship. A poor unfortunate lad of seven was buried here today, and his grave was watered by the tears of his loving and broken-hearted parents. It`s my job to see that his grave stays peaceful, tonight, and all nights."

"Good man!" said Hopwood. "Come George. It`s late enough. Let us return."

"Goodnight, sirs," said Canky.

Horseman of the Apocalypse, he muttered to himself, as he made his way back. Horseman of the Apocalypse, my arse!

By the time he caught up with the group, they had nearly reached the last turn of the winding ginnel at the foot of the Warren. It was here that Canky`s own house and yard stood, and though it was less than a hundred yards to the river, it was here that one of the most testing stages of the journey lay. The shorter way would have been to go directly to the bridge at John Lee Fold, but this would have involved passing two rows of cottages, where people might be stirring whatever the hour of the night. Lodge Street, which they now had to cross, and which connected Market Place to the Boarshaw road, was a place where late revellers, making their way home, and others out and about on some business of the night, might be met.

From the shadow of the ginnel besides Canky`s house, they peered out, this way towards the town, that way towards Boarshaw, and across towards the Tonge road. On this night, all was still. Bill Nimmy went on ahead, as far as the bridge, and then signalled back. The others, with their burden, now made their way, past the tithe barn and the edge of the parkland to the same spot, where, in the shadows beneath the bridge, the shallow barge lay waiting which was to carry them and their charge along the seven miles of river to their destination, the point in the heart of Manchester where the Irk reached its confluence with the Irwell.

The young lad who had been keeping the boat was now dismissed with his well-earned sixpence, and the five who had carried the body from the churchyard were now reduced to two or three. Canky himself seldom went with the boat, his main business being at the churchyard itself, both before and after, though occasionally, to show faith with his men, he took a turn.

Tonight, however, when they were settled, he helped push the boat off, and made his way back to the town with Scrat and Ned Small, leaving Sam Forcher and Bill Nimmy to steer the boat to its destination.

"What`s this about you and some hoor, then?" he asked Scrat when Ned Small had taken his own way down Lodge Street.

"What? Oh, nowt. It`s nowt."

"Not a Middleton lass, is it?"

"No. What do you tek me for?"

"Good. Never bring it to your own doorstep."

"It`s done wi`," Scrat retorted, impatiently, though inside he was thinking that Canky had never said a truer word.

They came to the gate of Canky`s house. "I`ll have a walk up as far as the church before I go in," said Canky. "Make sure all`s good and peaceful."

"Right," said Scrat, "I`ll mek my way home then."

He set out, in the opposite direction round the Warren, picking up the footpath which led upwards to his own house. The apprehension he felt as he approached it was the same he had been feeling, in one form or another, for the last two days, - that of finding Lucy Brindle waiting for him.

On the morning after, his first job of the day had been to go to the locksmith to buy a new padlock and chain, double the size of those which had previously secured his cellar door, and though there was nothing actually to be gained by this, as reason argued it, it nevertheless pleased him to feel that he was doing something to consolidate its privacy. At every turn of the street, however, he had feared bumping into Lucy.

"What do you want that padlock for, Scrat, and what do you want that chain for, Scrat?" he heard her saying. And then he heard her laughing. "You`ll need more than chains and locks to keep your secrets safe, Scrat, now that I know of `em."

The worst was passing the stile, opposite the Boar`s Head, which he had to do half a dozen times a day just carrying out his normal business. Each time, as he approached, he pictured her standing there, as she had the previous evening. "Hello, Joe, I`ll wager you remember me this time, don`t you!"

It was there that he had lingered earlier, telling the others he would catch them up. A little emboldened by drink, he had determined to have it out with her, to give her a good warning, if need be. But just as on the other occasions during the day, and just as now, as he hurriedly let himself in from the darkness of the night, and bolted the door behind him, she was not there.

Chapter 21

By the time Scrat had reached home, and by the time Canky had smoked a peaceful and satisfying pipe by the empty grave of Daniel Dyson, the boat which carried the latter to his appointment in Manchester, was gliding through Middleton Woods towards Rhodes. Alkrington Hall, high up on the hill above, with a few lights still twinkling even at this hour, was a familiar landmark to the midnight navigators. Here the river swung in an extravagant double curve, and then proceeded, more or less straight for a mile, under the shelter of hill and woodland. This was one of the easy stages of the journey. The river here was evenly deep, two to three feet, and fast flowing, so that no paddling was needed, just the occasional steer or push where the current took the vessel too near the bank.

It was during this part of the journey that the men sometimes talked, in hushed tones, partly to affirm the sense that all was going well, partly to offset the tensions which they knew lay ahead at places along the course they were following.

"What do you think they want this one for, then, Bill? I saw him with his father not long since. He was never but a bit of scrag-end, and misshapen with it. What good is he to them?"

"What good is any to them, come to that?"

"Aye, well, you`ve a point there, but as they pay good money, I warrant there must be some purpose."

"Well, I`ve heard it said that they take `em to some secret place, a labratry, or something like that, they call it, and they seek a way to bring them back to life."

"I`d like to know how they try that."

"It`s by science."

"And yet, I`ve never known anyone as was taken to Manchester by this route walk back into Middleton on his own legs to tell his folk that all`s well, and to stop grieving and drink a drink to Oliver Canky, have you?"

They sniggered at this, and then brooded for some time on the question they had asked. The boat slid on and Bill pushed his oar against the bank to reset its course again.

"What I believe the science of it is, or so I`ve heard, is that they cut the dead bodies up to make a study of them. They have a look at the liver and the lungs and the heart and so forth, with the idea of writing books, medical books, you know."

"Well good luck to them, I say."

"Sshh!" said Bill, suddenly. Of all the gang he was the one with the sharpest ears, and this was why Tom liked it when Bill was one of the boatmen.

They waited, tensely.

"It`s all right," whispered Bill, at last. "Nothing."

Nevertheless, they now progressed in silence. Rhodes, where there was sometimes some late night revelry was quiet tonight; they came, a short time later, to the hill of Heaton Hall, and there the river swung away to the left, under Hill Top Bank towards Blackley. In this section the river became wider, so that there were shallows and sand-banks, first on this side, then on the other, and it needed skill and concentration, to steer the right course so that the boat didn`t come stuck.

Blackley. Hazel Bottom. Collyhurst.

The closer they got to Manchester, the greater was the sense of danger. The settlements, with their occasional lights, were closer together, and there was a feeling, unspoken but shared, nevertheless, that there were men hereabouts that were of a desperate cut-throat nature.

"I`d be loath to set out to deliver a body and then be delivered myself," said Tom. "Science or no science."

At last, they came into the basin of Manchester, and pulled alongside the usual wharf, where they were met by the man with whom Canky did his dealings in the Boar`s Head. The little sack was transferred to a cart, and the cart departed from the wharf. As usual, they tied up the boat and left it, where, later, someone would come to deal with it. That was all part of the trade. Canky`s trade.

Not a word was spoken.

"What do you think, then," said Sam, as they made their way up through the maze of alleys between the river and the old Church, "shall we walk straight home, or seek out some pleasure of the town?"

"I don`t know," said Bill, "what do you think?"

A tinkling of laughter nearby, directed at them, which immediately became a double tinkling, persuaded them.

"Come on, then, let`s take a lesson out of Scrat`s testament."

Chapter 22

B yron was now in much better form.
      The midnight visit to the churchyard in Middleton had, he declared enthusiastically, stimulated his imagination and he had proposed another such outing before his departure, though he had not – and for this Robert Gregge Hopwood was grateful – alluded to it since.

His solicitor, Hanson had paid a visit that morning and reported progress.

"Of course," he said, "the title, Lord of the Manor of Rochdale, means little, the land concerned having already been ventured in commercial agreements which cannot entirely be recovered..."

"I`m not interested in the title," interrupted Byron. "I am not in need of more titles, I am in need of more capital."

"Quite so," said Hanson. "The legal quibble is this: your great uncle William entered into an agreement to sell Rochdale, which, though it was entered into freely on his part, was clearly fraudulent. Now, to prove this to the full satisfaction of the law is a matter of some complexity, and legal process can be a damnably expensive and protracted matter. The proper way to proceed, in my judgement, is to explore avenues where mutually beneficial compromises can be agreed."

"I don`t know why I don`t just leave you to deal with it and go back to London."

For a fleeting moment, Robert Gregge Hopwood found himself hoping – and it was an impulse for which he immediately reprimanded himself – that Hanson would agree that there might be more than a grain of common-sense in this proposal.

"Unfortunately, my lord," said Hanson, "the successful resolution, which I hope will be within three or four days, will require some signatures on your part."

Shortly after that, Hanson departed.

"Four days," Byron said. "Can I impose on your hospitality for that long, Robert? Perhaps I should take rooms at an inn. I don`t need much. I`m sure I can find somewhere that will serve."

"My dear George," he replied, "I wouldn`t dream of it! As long as you are in Lancashire, you are my guest, and you must treat this house as your own."

"Within reason, of course..." said Byron, with a perfectly mischievous grin. Then he laughed, loudly, and clapped him round the shoulders. "You`re a true friend, Robert. I can`t tell you how much that means to me. You know Matthews died, don`t you?"

"Yes, I`d heard."

"Poor Matthews. Drowned. Who would have thought it?"

"Life is sometimes cruel."

"I sometimes feel a curse hangs over me. First my mother, now Matthews."

There was a long pause in which Robert judged it best to let Byron indulge his thoughts. Then, as so often, his mood changed suddenly. "But do you remember London, Bob?"

"Indeed."

Byron gave out a huge laugh, throwing his head back. "Outrageous!" he said, as if this word alone, singly, could encapsulate the experience. "I don`t know how we got away with it!"

"How you got away with it, my lord!" Robert quipped.

"Do you remember my twenty-first, at Reddish`s on St James Street?"

"How could I forget it!"

"My coming-of-age. Do you know something, Bob, I thought that my coming-of-age would allow me to free up my assets.

Instead it just made me responsible for the debts I already had! What a world we live in! Hanson thinks I should sell Newstead, you know. He doesn`t say so openly but that`s what he believes. And you know why he won`t say it openly?"

"My lord?"

"Because he knows I won`t countenance it. A fig for his wise counsels! My dog`s buried at Newstead, and I intend to be buried there next to him. A dog`s friendship never alters or wavers, never has any conditions, do you know that?"

"I believe it to be true."

"My mother`s advice was that I should marry someone with two or three thousand a year. A wealthy dowdy to ennoble the dirty puddle of her mercantile blood by marriage to a baron. A golden Dolly. That`s what she was, you know. My father married her for her fortune and then blew it all away."

"You could do worse than making a good marriage."

"That`s probably how it will end. A golden Dolly or blow my brains out. Come to think of it, I think I might prefer blowing my brains out. Actually, you know, touching on what you said before, I didn`t get away with it."

"My lord?"

"I didn`t get away with it. I just went abroad!"

They both laughed heartily, though Robert Gregge Hopwood`s laughter was tinged, just a little, with nervousness.

Byron`s good humour, however, continued through to dinner-time, when, once again Cecilia and her younger sister formed an attentive audience.

"When I was at Cambridge," Byron declared, "I was greatly disappointed to find that the statutes forbade any student of the college to keep a dog, and so, instead, and Robert will confirm this, I kept a bear."

"It`s true," said Robert, laconically, as eyes turned to him.

"What, in your rooms?" asked Eleanor, the widest-eyed of all.

85

"Bruin," said Byron, "for so he was christened, occasionally visited my rooms, but no, he was generally kept at the stables where he and my horse kept company, but, and here`s the point, I intended to enter Bruin for a fellowship, sure in the knowledge that in point of intellect he would be the match of many who would have been his rivals, but alas, the jealousy of some who feared the competition prevented me from doing so."

"But tell us a little more," said Cecilia, when the ripple of mirth had subsided, "about the people amongst whom you travelled in your great excursion. In morals and manners, are they so very different from people here?"

Robert Gregge Hopwood detected a momentary look of weariness passing across Byron`s countenance, though in fairness, he also noticed that it was quickly suppressed.

"Tell us again about the Maid of Athens," said Eleanor. "Was she very beautiful?"

"Very beautiful," said Byron, "And very virtuous. Beautiful and virtuous."

There was an audible sigh from Eleanor, as if, in her innermost thoughts, she imagined Byron to be describing herself.

"But their religious practices are different, are they not?"

"To some extent, madam, they are."

"To what extent? Do they have Quakers and Conference Methodists, and Old Methodists or Kilhamite Methodists, or are they of the Church?"

"Perhaps they`re Catholics, Cecilia," suggested Eleanor, trying to show her breadth of knowledge.

"You`re perfectly right," said Byron, to Eleanor`s great pleasure. "In Portugal, and Spain, the old religion has never been broken by reform, quite the opposite. In Greece, a different form of Christianity is followed, as much at enmity with the church of Rome, as is the church of Rome with the church in England."

"I don`t see why they can`t all put their differences aside," said Cecilia.

"In Albania, however," Byron continued, "the populace is Muslim, as is the Ali Pasha himself, and their beliefs and customs are very different. They pray to Allah – very assiduously too – and their scripture is the book of the Koran, dictated by the prophet Mohammed himself."

There was a sense in the room that Byron had shown great courage in subjecting himself to the dangers implicit in exposure to such wicked things.

"They are," said Byron correcting an allusion to the Saracen and the Crusades, "a very gentle people and their religion is essentially one of peace. The crusades, like most wars, I fear, were a matter of adventure and conquest rather than religion. Besides, they happened a long time ago."

Robert nodded to Burley who went round the table offering more wine to those who wanted it.

"Is it true," asked Cecilia, "that the Mohammedan may take more than one wife?"

"The Ali Pasha has two hundred wives," said Byron, causing something of a gasp. "He is a despot, however, albeit a kindly one, but yes, in matrimonial matters, differences abound. For example, when a girl passes into womanhood, she must not be seen by men, but must stay hidden at home or cover her face entirely with a veil. Consequently, when a man and a woman marry, as their fathers determine it, they will never have seen each other until the day of their wedding."

This caused another gasp.

"But what if they don`t love each other," said Eleanor, horrified, "or even like each other?"

"Well, then," said Byron, after the briefest of pauses, "I suppose they must find themselves in the same predicament as many English husbands and wives."

The joke was well taken, and as the laughter and chatter continued, Robert Gregge Hopwood, who had been momentarily a little twitchy when the conversation began to touch on sexual mores, now, and with the help of a few more sips of wine, reassured himself that the evening was going well, and that the few remaining days of Byron`s stay would pass off without any unpleasantness.

Cecilia had certainly changed her tune, and she was even now proposing the *soiree* she had envisaged when their guest first arrived.

Damn those curling auburn locks, said Gregge Hopwood to himself, though not without an inward smile, and damn that pale luminous complexion! She wants to show him off! I do believe she`s infatuated with the scoundrel again!

Chapter 23

With regular sleep and decent wholesome food and abstinence from strong drink, Lucy Brindle soon appeared to be fulfilling the hopes of those who took pains over her welfare. The bruise under her left eye had all but now healed, her complexion had softened, and her hair, neatly arranged each day, had regained some of the sheen it had had in the happier days of her youth.

She was passive and courteous to all in the house, and tried to make herself useful in small ways. Under Simon`s patient tuition, she attempted to master the art of winding the bobbins and they smiled together at her lapses, for often the spindle was turning faster than her hand could feed the thread.

"It`s always like that when you`re getting started," Simon reassured her.

She tried again and became a little better, but in truth her concentration did not last long, and most often she would tell him to take over and carry on so that she could watch and learn.

It was in young Simon`s company that she seemed to find most solace. If, during her first night in the house, it was a glimpse of him, and not merely a feverish hallucination which created the illusion of an angelic vision, his presence continued, it seemed, albeit in a less beatific way, to give her comfort.

"They`re almost like children together," Mima said to Sam, one morning. "They laugh and smile together, like brother and sister. I think they`re good for each other."

Sam nodded. Personally, he found it enough to have one odd character to deal with in the house, but what Mima said was true. Even after a few days, there seemed to be a bond between them, perhaps the bond between people who have known what it is to be a victim.

"When I was in Manchester, last bearing-home day," he said, changing the subject, "some of the chaps were talking about bad feeling mounting up over Ezekiel Barton`s mill down the road there."

"How so?"

"Fear of him cornering the trade, I suppose. Driving down the price."

"It`s only one small mill."

"It`s one small mill now, but where there`s one today there can be two tomorrow and that`s the thin end of the chock driven in."

"We`ve had mills before, in the woollen trade, and it never stopped folk weaving for a living at home."

"No, but these are power-looms and they say an engine can do the work of a dozen men."

"I`d like to see the quality of an engine`s warp and weft."

"Aye, well, that`s as may be. We`ll have to wait and see what comes of it."

"Well, I hope there`ll be no trouble over it, anyroad."

After supper, they all sat together in the back kitchen and Sam read from Dean Swift`s book of Gulliver`s Travels which he had found on the penny market in Manchester. Apart from Lucy, whose eyes closed intermittently with the enticement of sleep, they all listened enthralled, laughing at the wonderful absurdities of the Lilliputian nobility.

"Is there really a place where there are tiny people like that?" asked Jack, the little one.

"A book can make you believe almost anything," said Sam.

"But in real life?"

"I don`t know about that, but I do know that in real life it`s time for you to be in bed."

"That was nice," said Mima, afterwards.

"I`ve always loved the magic of books," he said. "I fancy I might try to make some more verse of my own next time we`re slack. Not that I`m wishing that on us!"

"I heard say that Squire Hopwood has a poet staying with the family at the hall. Lord something or other."

Sam shrugged.

"Maybe you should show him some of your rhymes and see about getting them printed in a book."

"If he`s a lord, he`ll not be interested in what a Middleton weaver puts on paper. He`d not understand the dialect for a start!"

Mima laughed, and Sam started to fill his pipe.

"Why don`t you take your pipe down to the Boar`s Head for an hour?" she said.

"Don`t you mind?"

"You`ve not been for nearly a week. Go on. You deserve it."

It was a pleasant night for a walk out. Rather than go directly, for in fact the Boar`s Head was no more than quarter of a mile down the road, he walked up towards Barrowfield and then followed the path which skirted the graveyard towards St Leonard`s. In the gloom of twilight, all was quiet and peaceful across the graves, though he recalled, sadly, that poor young Daniel, the blacksmith`s lad, had been buried there not two days before. Death was everywhere. Barrowfield itself, they said, was so named because it had been, in the ancient times, a place of burial. He shivered, and, picking out the warm light at the windows of the Boar`s Head below, quickened his pace.

In the public house, it was one of those desultory nights when people were sitting in ones and twos, talking quietly, in private conversation.

"Evening Sam," said one.

"Evening Sam," said another.

But it was not one of those convivial nights when he, or anyone else, would be urged on to get up and tell a tale, or sing a song. He furnished himself with some ale, and finding a broadsheet which someone had left, sat down in a corner to read it, and lit his pipe.

What made him look up, he wasn't sure. He wasn't even sure how long he'd been sitting there, except that he'd been enjoying a witty piece of satire about a doddering old magistrate and that he was just about ready for a second mug of ale; but when he did look up, the man he saw across the bar, talking to the landlord, was one he immediately recognised. It was not a Middleton man, however, or one he knew by way of trade, here, or in Manchester, or anywhere else. The man he recognised belonged to a pocket of memory linked to the Greenfield district of Manchester some years before. It was the man who, as he escaped from the dark alley where he had experienced the shock of recognising Lucy Brindle, had tried to accost him. It was the man who, as he had continued his flight, he had left measuring his length against the cobbles of the pavement.

"Not seen that one before," he said to Will Robin, the landlord, when the man had gone. "What's his business, then?"

"Looking for a woman of his acquaintance. Said she'd come to meet someone hereabouts. Said she owed him money. Well, you know what that adds up to, don't you?"

"Who was it, then, did he say?"

"Well, he said this, and he said that, and he said she might go by the name of Lucy or she might go by the name of Dolly, but that she was probably wearing a crimson jacket and skirt and bonnet with a feather. And had I seen her?"

"Not much to go on."

"Well, Sam, that's not the point. I might have seen her, and I might not have seen her; I see a lot of people, but what I let slip about them, I keep wary of. It comes down to this, Sam. We don't want his type round here. That's what I concluded, so I denied all knowledge, whether I had any, or whether I had any not."

"I reckon you did the right thing, Will. Have one with me."

"That`s very kind of you, Sam. I`ll just top this one up then and wish you the best of health."

Returning to his table, he folded the broadsheet and put it to one side. Now, Sam Bamford, he said to himself, the question is this: what`s to do now? Ought or nought.

Sipping his ale slowly he began to ponder the possible consequences of each.

Chapter 24

"**S**urely, he`s not going to desert us at this stage!" said Cecilia. "Does he not realise how far the preparations have gone!"

"Who am I to predict his moods?" said Robert, feeling, once again caught between the upper and the nether, that his noble guest was more a nuisance than an adornment.

Byron had declared, that morning, that he was going to go back, directly, to London.

"There`s nothing else for it. It`s dragging on and on. Hanson`s made a mess of it. I`ll have to raise a mortgage on Newstead."

The only relief was that he had not gone yet.

"Twenty guests," said Cecilia, "twenty guests and now he says he`s going back to London."

"I`ll speak to him," said Robert, vaguely and wearily aware that he had said such a thing before.

He found Byron by the river, sitting on a stone near the bridge. It had become one of his favourite haunts when alone.

"I hope I`m not disturbing your contemplation," said Robert, approaching. Byron gestured with his hand, inviting him to sit.

"I like this spot," he said. "It has a tranquillity which is very English. I hate most things English, but this combination of leafiness and water and mild sunshine, I like."

"In your letter," said Robert, "you mentioned a poem..."

"I scribbled some doggerel during my travels, Childe Harold's Pilgrimage."

"Childe Harold being?"

"A blackguard like myself?"

"That`s not what I said, or what I intended to say..."

"Well, then, let me answer – even more of a blackguard than myself. But no, I`m minded to abandon the project."

"How so?"

"I`m done with scribblement as a profession. Murray`s keen for me to continue, but then he would be, a publisher with a nose for business. But no. I`m done with all that. When I`ve sorted out my finances, by whatever means necessary, I shall devote myself to the restoration of Newstead, and to politics or some such thing. Eddlestone joined the army, you know. I`ve considered that myself. I rather like the splendour of the uniforms. They don`t compare with Albanian costume, which is superb, but I like to dress up and shoot guns, so I might make a tolerable lieutenant colonel."

"But tell me, George, what is it that you hate about things English?"

"The cant, the hypocrisy, the narrow-mindedness, the bigotry – how long do you want me to go on for?"

"You mentioned Matthews to me the other day."

"Yes, poor Matthews. What a waste!"

"There was a rumour, and only a rumour I must emphasise, that Matthews` death was a suicide bid which he attempted to abandon, though unfortunately, too late."

"He was caught up in the weeds. Both his legs and his arms."

"The rumour also alluded to a case of sodomy which was to be brought against him."

Byron stood, suddenly, in agitation, and threw a handful of the sandy gravel into the river, then, just as suddenly, sat down again.

"Listen, George, there`s something I want to say, but not a word of this in the house, mind you. All that talk, in Cambridge and London, you know, all that high-spirited nonsense about lightly bounding boys, about Ganymedes and Hyacinths, and what not, it was all very well in those circles, but in the real world, it`s dangerous."

"Do you think I don`t know that?"

"No. But you`ve been abroad. It changes the way people see things. I just want you to be careful."

"The English Education system is based on the Classics, both Greek and Roman, which abound, as you well know, in tales of the *eromenos*, the beautiful youth, pursued by Gods to serve their heroic lust, or for gentler sexual pleasures, or merely for friendship and adoration, but yet at the least whiff of scandal, the English cry `buggery` and gloat with satisfaction that they have turned it into a capital offence. That`s what I meant just now by hypocrisy!"

"I don`t make the laws, George, but what I do say…"

"What is it Lear says? *Thou rascal beadle, hold thy bloody hand! Why dost thou lash that whore? Strip thine own back, that hotly lust'st to use her in that kind for which thou whipp'st her.* Hypocrisy."

"Quite so," said Robert. "Though I`m sure I don`t need to point out, that the object of lust in this case, is, in fact, if we are to believe the pronouns, a woman."

Byron guffawed loudly. "You always were a pedant and a plodder, Robert," he laughed, slapping him on the back. "You`re quite right, of course, but if you read the sonnets, I think you might conclude that the greatest English bard of all wasn`t beyond a bit of Ganymeding, after all."

"No, I suppose not."

"It`s rife in the theatre anyway. Always has been."

"So, tell me, did you find Greece as you expected, in this respect?"

"The culture is more tolerant. They don`t have such precious and high-minded notions of their own moral superiority."

Robert Gregge Hopwood found himself nodding.

"A youth may find his way out of poverty by the generosity of an appreciative patron. So might a girl, you will argue, quite rightly, but a girl may, nay probably will, become pregnant, so then there`s a problem, as I know full well myself. Then, you

96

may say, there is the danger of the clap, but to be truthful, the clap is no great respecter of gender. It will go where it will go, though it will never go, and of this, my dear friend Robert, I am absolutely sure, into the precincts of Hopwood Hall."

"I should hope not," said Robert, with deliberately ironic timorousness."

Byron laughed, heartily.

"By the way," said Robert, a short time later, and remembering his initial purpose. "Cecilia asked me to mention the *soiree* she`s arranged for tomorrow..."

"Of course," said Byron, "how could I forget?"

"Then you won`t be departing for London today?"

"Of course not. What on earth put that idea in your head?"

"It must have been a misunderstanding."

"Besides, I haven`t had my second ride out at midnight yet, Robert. Don`t forget that!"

"No," said Robert Gregge Hopwood, with an inwardly drawn sigh.

Chapter 25

Regarding a certain person, seen in a public house, asking questions about a certain other person, Sam Bamford had decided to say nothing. No good could come of it, he reasoned. It would raise anxiety where at the moment there was calm; it would argue the possibility of a cause of alarm without putting anyone in a position to do anything about it. As things were, Lucy never left the house, and though the neighbours knew they were looking after an unfortunate friend, no-one had any cause to link her with the bedraggled and tarnished specimen who had turned up, a week ago, seeking the whereabouts of Joe Howarth.

So far so good.

If the fellow were to be seen loitering he would soon be reported as a malingerer and the constable would see that he was dealt with. More likely, he would have cut his losses and moved on; if, as he suspected, Lucy was, to use the Manchester vernacular, his `fancy pal` and he her `bully`, there would no doubt be other girls willing enough to put themselves under his protection, if one left the fold. He would soon be drawn back to the back streets and cellars and dark alleys of Manchester which were his proper habitat.

Sam Bamford, to conclude, decided to keep a sharp eye open, but otherwise to get on with life as normal, and once he had made it, it was a decision he was happy with.

Lucy, meantime, in the judgement of those who kept a careful watch over her, was making as much progress as could be hoped for. Whether she sat gazing into the fire, or sat gazing at Simon as he worked – for the original impression he had made on her seemed undiminished – she was as placid as a lamb. It was as if, Mima ventured to suggest, she was bit by bit regaining the sweetness of temper which was her true nature, and which she had only lost through the attrition of bad fortune. In her true nature, of course, it was possible that she might have been a little less prone to passivity than she now was, but in time, with help, she would rediscover the satisfaction that goes with honest hard work and activity.

Under the still surface, however, of Lucy`s tranquillity, quite a long way beneath it, in fact, far enough below to be completely invisible to benign watchfulness, deeper currents were beginning to stir.

To begin with, in these lower precincts of her consciousness, she was beginning to develop a powerful thirst. To one used to being soused in drink for the most part of every day, the first few days of abstinence, and with it freedom from the oppressive and lugubrious after-effects of drink, had been like the pleasure of redemption, a deliverance from evil. Then, because it seemed that temperance was so much its own reward that one could never imagine voluntarily choosing anything else, it had seemed possible to recollect, without danger, the warming effect of a tot of rum, the stream of happiness of a few gin swizzles, the fiery companionship of a slowly sipped brandy.

From this, it was only a short step to thinking that if it was possible to slip away from this place of virtue and blessedness, for she truly believed it to be so, for a short time and a little bit of fun, no real harm would come of it.

It was usually in the evening, when Sam was reading aloud from one of his books, from Rasselas, or Gulliver, or Pilgrim`s Progress that these thoughts came most strongly upon her, and as they did so, the course of events which had brought her back to Middleton also returned to preoccupy her thoughts. She was used to dealing with toss-pots who lost their cock half-way through, but Joe, the chap they called Scrat had come up from his business down by the river, whatever that was, sober as a judge, and keen as he was, he`d given her a proper one, that was for sure.

"If I ever hear you going off like that again," said Skinner, who`d been standing by, "I`ll spoil your face for you."

"That`s how they like it, you know that."

"Don`t tell me what I know."

"That`s how you like it, anyway, though there`s not a man alive who really knows if it`s real or if it`s put on, and that includes you, Skinner."

This had caused much mirth in the company they were then in, and it was for this, the next morning, that she had received the bruise under her eye which, two days later, she had brought with her to Middleton.

What Skinner didn`t know was that later in the evening, in another drinking house, she had met up with Scrat again, now very much in his cups.

"You`re a Middleton lass, then, Lucy," he said.

"When time was."

"Well, I'm a Middleton man, through and through. And any time you want to come to Middleton, just ask for me, and you`ll be reet."

"Right, I will then," she said.

What she`d hoped to gain by coming to Middleton in search of him, apart from getting away from Skinner, she didn`t really know. It certainly wasn`t the two half-crowns because she could have doubled that with an easy night`s work in Manchester. The whole thing was probably nothing more than a whim. And now here she was, sitting in the midst of these good people, listening to tales of virtue trying to triumph over evil, and the Christian soul progressing bravely through the Slough of Despond. She certainly hadn`t bargained for that, any more than she had bargained for what she`d come across, in the flickering light of a candle, in Scrat`s cellar.

Arriving at the house, he had barred and locked the main door, then he had boasted that where he was, positioned up on the top of the Warren, he could see the whole of Middleton below, on three sides, adding that he had a garret upstairs with a powerful spy-glass, as well - in case he saw anything that needed looking into more closely, he joked. Next he said he`d get them a tipple, to see them on their way, and that was when she`s seen him take the key from round his neck to unfasten the padlock on the cellar door. She had no desire to follow him down there, so she`d waited in the kitchen until he came back, a few minutes later, clutching a dusty bottle of what he called Bonaparte`s own finest.

"Here, try that," he said, pouring some into a little glass cup, "and tell me what you think."

"Nice," she said, "very nice."

It was true. The taste was mellow and easy on the tongue, and then it expanded into refined glow at the back of the throat sending soft flames into the blood.

"Very nice!"

There was a world of difference between that and some of the rough scorchers that were served up for brandy in the places where she usually took her liquor.

"Come on, then," he said, "we`ll take it upstairs with us."

Upstairs, he had a cupful himself, which he knocked back quickly, and then he offered her another drop – there seemed only to be one of the glass cups – and then kicked off his boots and his breeches, blew out the candle and got into bed.

"Come on," he said. "Be sharp."

In the normal way of business, she had to do little more than hoist up her skirts, but now, for the novelty of it, she undressed down to her shift, and got into bed beside him.

He wasn`t up to much, and that was a fact. At the outset, you would have thought him Hercules, setting out on his thirteenth and greatest labour, but after two minutes he was huffing and puffing, and sweating and muttering, and getting – if she was any judge – nowhere. A further two minutes and he`d fallen asleep on top of her and it was all she could do to bundle him off. A few minutes later and his snoring was coming deep and steady, so that was that.

There was enough moonlight coming into the room, with her eyes now adjusted anyway, to see where her garments lay on the side of a chair, so, not wanting to lie there listening to him snoring all night, she got up, dressed, and went downstairs. There, she made herself comfortable in a chair, and had it in mind to doze for an hour or two until the first light, and then let herself out. She checked that the two half-crowns were safely tucked away in her purse, and then hid it, as usual when there was anything in it, on the inside of her skirt. She recalled that Scrat had put his own wallet on the bedside chair and it did occur to her that she could easily go back and pay herself even more handsomely, but she decided not to. It wasn`t her fault that he hadn`t taken proper delivery of the goods he`d paid for, but she`d got a crown and a night`s lodging, so fair was fair enough.

What she was less fastidious about was the bottle of Bonaparte`s finest which was still on the table in his chamber, so upstairs she went again and brought it down along with the little glass cup. When she next opened her eyes, she was sitting in the armchair and the light of dawn was beginning to filter into the house. The little glass cup was resting in her lap and the bottle of Bonaparte, now somewhat diminished, was beside her. A further half-cup served to drive off the malevolent symptoms which had gathered as she dozed, and she was about to put on her bonnet and let herself out, when it struck her that it would probably be no great loss to Scrat if she were to take a bottle or two of the Bonaparte with her. A gratuity.

Upstairs she went again.

Scrat had kicked off the bed covers in the night and was now lying naked on his back – and a pitiful sight it made, too – but it was no great difficulty to ease the string with the key from round his neck. Then she pulled the sheet up, to cover his paltry shame, went downstairs, opened the padlock, lit a candle and picked her way down the steep narrow steps which led down to the cellar.

It was easy to see where Scrat kept his liquor. There were bottles of it, racked up along the wall, there were casks of it, settled on small wooden sleepers and as yet untapped, and then, on another wall, there were bottles again, and all of them softly woven about by the spider`s careful work. A bottle or two of Bonaparte, she thought, would certainly not be missed.

But this, she realised, was just one room, and beyond it a door led to another room and that room led to another stairway which descended lower. Intrigued, Lucy held the candle in front of her and followed its light...

"Are you all right, Lucy?"

It was Mima`s voice.

"Yes," she muttered, her voice so dry and faint it could hardly be heard.

"You were staring so intently in front of you, you seemed in a trance."

"I was just thinking how kind providence has been, to bring me here, undeserving as I am, to a hearth so filled with kindness and love."

Mima squeezed her hand and smiled.

Over Mima`s shoulder, she could see the face of Simon, so pure and beautiful, it seemed, and yet with eyes that seemed to peer down through her own into the very depths of her soul, and to know everything, good, bad, or merely chaotic, that resided there.

Chapter 26

S crat, in his youth, had been set on to work with the saddler
of the Lord of the Manor, Ralph Assheton, the father of the
present Lady Suffield. He was not a great one for horses, but he
liked working with the tackle, and what he particularly liked
was watching his master, Bob Stiles, working with the leather.

"What you have to remember," said Bob, "when you`re
working with leather, is that you`re working with a living skin,
well, a skin that has been living until recently, and which still
has a lot of the properties of a living skin. It has to be cured, so
that it doesn`t go rotten like a corpse, and then it has to be
looked after with the right oils and ointments and polishes,
and then it`ll stay as soft and supple and moist as the inside of
a maiden`s thigh, and when you find out what that feels like,
you`ll be able to tell me I was right."

All this, and other encomiums on the qualities of leather,
whilst he was polishing, rubbing, and sometimes sewing with a
long needle and stiff twine, formed Scrat`s instruction and the
lad was keen to learn.

One day, having some business with his fellow at the stables
at Alkrington Hall, Bob allowed young Scrat to accompany him,
and whilst they were there, Scrat was shown the collection of
exotic curios which formed the `museum` of Sir Ashton Lever.
There were, in this collection, items from around the world
which might excite the curiosity of any youngster –
tomahawks, scalping knives, shrunken heads, sections from
carved totem poles, spears, strings of shark`s teeth, but what
captured Scrat`s imagination most was the collection of stuffed
rare and exotic animals, including a squirrel monkey, an arctic
fox, a flamingo, a bird of paradise, fish, snakes, and so it went
on.

Amongst the preparations used at the local tannery, with which the saddler had frequent business, were arsenic, realgar and orpiment, all used in the preparation and preservation of hides and skins, and by dint of questioning him, Scrat discovered that the application of arsenic soap was the best way of preventing the deterioration, through decay, of the softer skins and furs of such creatures as mice, voles, even cats, and he began his own experiments – not always very successful, to begin with - in the art of taxidermy.

He purchased, from a stall on the new market which dealt with bric-a-brac, a set of surgeon`s scalpels which had somehow found their way there; needles and thread were readily available at the stables, and the rest was largely a matter of improvisation. It was important to get rid of as much of the perishable matter as possible, this was the first lesson Scrat learned. Whether it was a cat or a puppy, a rat or a rabbit, the heart, the liver, the muscle, the stomach, the cortex – all had to go. So, too – leaving aside the skull - the skeleton, which was a pity, as the skeleton it was which most obviously defined the creature, but it was difficult to keep a skeleton intact, and even if you managed to do so, it would last only three or six months before its own soft and adhesive parts deteriorated, and it collapsed. The inner form and rigidity had to be achieved by other artificial means. As did such obvious external features as the eyes. Gradually, Scrat`s proficiency and his knowledge increased.

It was at about this time, when he was seventeen or eighteen, that Scrat fell in love with the daughter of a gentleman farmer who lived in the Birch area. It was at the Wakes, in August, when each fold or hamlet in the parish prepared a cart to take to the church for the `rush-bearing`. It was a time for rivalry, mainly good natured, though not always so, but in the main it was a great festive occasion, with the lads and the lasses dressing up in new clothes they`d saved up for during the year, and with plenty of music and dancing up and down the town. Amidst the heady festivity, and in the good-natured banter and fun, the young Scrat found himself exchanging glances, at first bashfully fleeting, and then more confidently prolonged, with the lass in question, and after the sports on the green, where he had done his best to show off for her benefit, he had made his approach, and she had not disdained it. She was called Dorothea, a name which, to Scrat, immediately took on the most romantic connotations, and he cared not that the other lads mocked his dalliance, because his heart was dancing, and he was head-over-heels in love.

That she was above his station, and therefore above his hope, Scrat well knew. But a young man in love will gladly bang his head against reality, even to the point of dashing his own brains out. When work was done, Scrat would walk four miles each day along the lanes to Birch, just so he would not miss the opportunity of telling her, should she be able to slip away from the house to meet him, how much he cared for her. She, managing to slip away from the house, at least two or three times a week, assured him that she cared for him, too. And so, three times happy, and four times not, Scrat walked the four miles back to Middleton, wondering what would become of them, but certain, as any man in the grip of a powerful infatuation is, that it would be something.

One Sunday, when her parents were visiting relatives in Bury, they walked out together, along the lanes and bridle paths by the side of fields, almost as far as Heaton Hall. It was a perfect day, just at the start of October, warm, and with a fine light irradiating the leaves, just beginning to get a hint of gold, and the red berries of the rowan trees. She let him hold her hand as they walked, and it seemed to young Scrat that he was being permitted a glimpse of paradise.

On their return, Dorothea became melancholy and tearful and Scrat supposed that it was because they must soon part. She told him, however, that her little pup, Jasmine, had died the previous day, and as they approached the farmhouse, she showed him the place where the unfortunate creature lay buried. At first he was a little disappointed that it was a lap-dog and not himself that was the cause of this show of feeling, but after bidding each other a fond farewell, he had not gone many paces on his way home, when an idea came to him. Retracing his steps to the place she had shown him, which was sheltered from the view of the house by a dense hedgerow, he scooped away the soil and retrieved the small carcass from the earth in which it was newly lain. The rigor-mortis was set in, but the fur, once the crumbs of soil had been brushed away, was still soft – as if finely combed by its mistress in preparation for eternal rest – and there were few other signs of outward corruption. He slipped it into the inside of his jacket, took it home, and immediately set about his work.

To present her with a mounted version of her beloved Jasmine, as true to life as when she had lain against her mistress' snowy bosom, arranged in a playful attitude, so that you might almost fancy you heard the little joyous yelp – this was his idea. It would be his master-piece.

Before it could be completed, however – the very next week, in fact – she told him that, as a result of her parents' visit to Bury, she was now being paid court to by Sir Robert Edgeworth, of Heywood, and that it was firmly expected of her that she should marry him.

"It'll only be for form," she reassured him. "We shan't love each other, it will always be you I truly love."

How could she say this with such blandness, such lightness? He wanted to open his throat and bellow his protest to the cruel heavens – but she put her finger to her lip and looked back over her shoulder.

"Don't be too sad, Joe," she said, at last, and in the same tone of almost blithe acceptance. "You'll see me at church, still. I'll drop a glove and you can be the gallant who picks it up for me."

A moment later, a voice came from the house, calling her name.

"I have to go," she said, and kissing her three fingertips together, she placed them against his lips, and then turned to go.

"You`ll soon get over her," said his friend, Oliver Canky, in the old Church Tavern, built right up against the wall of the churchyard itself. Canky had been a grave-digger for four years, and was ambitious to be sexton when old Ned Appleyard had run his course, which wouldn`t be long, Canky hoped. "I`ve always said, no good`ll ever come of it when lads like you and me go chasing after a silk stocking. Prissy little miss that she is, she`d probably die of shock if she saw what you were after bringing out of your breeches for her."

"All right, Canky, that`ll do!"

"If she could see what you had ready to split her kipper with."

"Any more, Canky, and I swear I`ll brain you with this pot."

"All right, all right, keep your wig on."

They sat for a time in a meditative silence; Canky, himself recently married, had some reflections of his own on the subject with which he`d tried to cheer his crony up with crude laughter. At last, he got up and recharged their pots. Scrat did not object.

"Here`s summat I heard, when I was in Manchester last, might interest you."

"If it`s about hoors I`m not interested."

Scrat knew why Canky went up to Manchester.

"It`s not. Well, I dare say some might find their way into the tale, but what I heard, talking to a chap there had nothing to do with hoors."

"Go on, then."

"No, this chap I was talking to is a man in the medical business."

"A doctor."

"Well, not so much a doctor, more a student at the college of medicine, a student of anatomy, and very interested he was when I told him my profession."

"How so?"

"Well, he was telling me of a surgeon in Bristol recently prosecuted for performing dissection on a corpse obtained by foul means from a local churchyard."

"Why should that interest me?"

"Well, you're a dissector, aren't you?"

"I'm a dissector of cats and voles, to stuff them."

And lap-dogs, he might have added, for the pelt of little Jasmine, lovingly rubbed with arsenical soap, was still awaiting the reconstructive craftsmanship which he had promised. It reminded him of everything about Dorothea that he was trying to forget.

"And he told me next," Canky went on, "of a sexton in Weaste who'd been before the magistrate for being caught perpetrating a similar deed. And the thing is, Joe, and this is what I'm coming to, he was telling me this, knowing I was a gravedigger, wondering how I would react, would I be shocked, and when I wasn't, do you know what he said? He said, I wager you'd be a bit more careful if it was you, wouldn't you, and I said, you could stake your life on me being more careful, if it was me, and with that he gave me a slip of paper with a man's name on it, and an address in Strangeways, and he said that should I ever wish to extend the scope of my profession I should go to this man at this house in Strangeways, and have a meeting of minds, that's how he put it, a meeting of minds."

"So, what are you telling me this for?"

"Well, I couldn't do it on my own, could I?"

Scrat looked up from his pot.

"You're not including me in this, I hope."

"I'm not including anyone. I'm not even including myself. I'm simply trying to find a means of diverting a lovelorn friend from his overblown preoccupation with a pretty face and a fancy petticoat."

"All right, then," said Scrat, enlivened by the ale, and deciding now to throw melancholy to the winds, "get another pot in, and we`ll put our two heads together, purely for diversion, and have a think about how it might be done."

Chapter 27

It was about six months after he had been jilted by Dorothea that Scrat found himself without a master. The old man`s wife had died, and the saddler, now nearing his threescore and ten, decided to retire to a small cottage in Thornham, near to an inn which was kept by his nephew. He was not replaced. Since the death of Sir Ralph, and with the new Squire, Lord Sutton and his wife, Mary, Sir Ralph`s daughter spending so much time in Norfolk and London, it was deemed an extravagance to keep a saddler when the one serving the town might suffice just as well, as and when required. It wasn`t just the stable, either; the whole household was reduced, and Scrat counted himself lucky to be kept on at all. He was made into something of an odd-job-man about the hall and its grounds. He didn`t touch the gardens, because the head gardener, Fitton, had very strict ideas about that, but anything else he would turn his hand to. He could knock in a nail here and there, mend a fence or stop a door creaking; he could polish the carriage which was kept for Lord Suffield`s aperiodic visits, and could look after its tackle. He could unblock chimneys, and get rid of birds` nests, lop dead branches from trees and chop logs; and he could set traps for mice and rats and other vermin which sometimes, in the absence of Lord and Lady Suffield, tried to take up residence there themselves. He was handy at most things, and it was owing to this, at about this time, that he acquired his nickname, when someone joked that he was always scratting about looking for odd jobs. Of course, it was young Scrat in those days, but the name stuck, spreading beyond the hall so that soon it was the one by which he was generally known.

It was on a clear fine day in March, almost a year after the old saddler`s departure, that Scrat was up on the roof of the hall, repairing some damage to tiles caused by heavy snows and frost the previous month, when, standing by the parapet to take a breather, he happened to glance over towards the Warren, where, set amongst high trees, still now in their winter nudity, stood the old house which the saddler and his wife had inhabited. A week later, when it so chanced that his lordship paid a visit, Scrat enquired if his lordship would like him to take some care of the place, to prevent it falling into dilapidation and becoming, vacant as it was, a victim of the seasons. His lordship, seeming to have little knowledge that the old house was in his estate – and even less interest – answered amicably that he might do with it as he saw fit.

Scrat took him at his word.

Over a period of two or three months, he secured the doors and shutters, swept out the detritus and leavings of opportunistic wild creatures, cleared the chimneys and lit fires to counteract the damp, cleaned and mopped the floors, mended some furniture, threw out the rest, or burnt it, and began to move in some pieces of his own. At what point Scrat actually moved in to live there, no-one, with the possible exception of Oliver Canky, knew; the fact that he did live there was something which seemed to seep only slowly into common realisation, but by the time it was firmly lodged there, no-one questioned it. It seemed that Scrat, a little bit odd as he was, and the old house, a little bit queer as it was, were perfectly matched; as if they were meant for each other.

Chapter 28

Sir Robert Edgeworth walked down the aisle of St Leonard`s with his bride, Dorothea, at about the same time that Scrat was beginning to refurbish his newly acquired house on the Warren. That she was a beautiful bride, no-one doubted. Radiant and caught up in her own spell-binding moment, she moved her head, slightly, from side to side, as she approached the altar, as if to spread the benign rays of her happiness to all who came within the circumference of her gaze. She did not see that Scrat was there, or if she did, she gazed through him.

Two days later, Canky and Scrat ferried the first of their bodies, their cadavers, as the man from Strangeways called them, down to Manchester and the confluence of the Irk and the Irwell, where their business was swiftly and discretely concluded.

"I'll do it once and once only," said Scrat, perturbed at how easily, when he'd had a few in the Church or the Boar`s head, he could be persuaded by Oliver Canky to do things which were against his better judgement.

And at the time he said it, he meant it.

Leaving aside the moral aspect of it, and leaving aside the legal aspect of it – getting caught and prosecuted, that is – he could think of nothing more lugubrious or gruesome than to be doing with the digging up of corpses in shadowy graveyards in the middle of the night. Indeed, the night before it was planned to happen, he had such ghoulish and hag-ridden dreams that he nearly went to see Canky that morning to give back word.

Once and once only.

It had to be said that Canky had a cool head and nerves of steel. At moments when Scrat felt his gut lurching with panic, or the blood draining out of his legs so that they hardly had the power to support him, Canky never faltered. When they were walking from the river past the old church and towards the town, Canky said, with a kind of brisk sniff, "I enjoyed that."

At first, Scrat was appalled by this, feeling, for his own part, only an immense relief that the filthy job, with all its dangers, was done, and that the body, already giving off more than a faint hint that the process of putrefaction had commenced, was now someone else's responsibility.

"Enjoyed it!" he expostulated.

They found a tavern at the corner of Old Mill Gate, The Black Boy, and quaffed two tankards without exchanging a word of conversation. Then they sat at a table in the corner, with a bottle, and Canky had a bright look about the eye, for all the world like someone enjoying a good night out.

"Do you know what I'm hankering after now, Scrat?" he said. "I'm hankering after some female company."

"Well, sup up then. We've a six mile walk ahead of us, and then you can have the company of your wife."

"Much joy may I have of her company!" said Canky, acerbically, for at that time it was still the first Mrs Canky of whom they spoke.

Nevertheless, when they had finished the liquor, they set off towards home, and were back in Middleton by three in the morning. And the strange thing was that when he began to look back on it, what Scrat remembered was not the unspeakable nature of the deed, in the eyes of God and man, but the thrill and the danger, the moments of heart-stopping apprehension, and, finally, the elation of safety, so that when he next saw Oliver Canky he was prompted to confess that he had enjoyed the venture, too.

"The gentleman from Strangeways likes our work," said Canky, two or three weeks later, "and he is minded to commission more of the commodity. What do you say, Scrat? Is it still to be once and once only, or are you in?"

Scrat took a sip of his brandy, and felt the fire of the liquor meeting the flame of excitement which had sprung up in his breast.

"Count me in," he said.

And it was in this way, with Scrat as his accomplice, that Canky`s trade began.

It was a remunerative, trade, too. Sufficiently remunerative for Scrat to fit out his cellar with racks and to fill those racks with his favourite bottles: French wines that were pleasant to drink with his food, rum from Jamaica, rich and dark, the best warmer on a winter morning, and his favourite of all, the one which conveyed him happily into the welcoming arms of Morpheus, his finest Bonaparte.

It was a trade of demand and supply which Canky and the gentleman from Strangeways endeavoured to keep in a sensible balance. The `commodity` was not required every week, nor even every month, but it was required enough, and a good, reliable, trustworthy supplier, especially in the kind of trade with which the gentleman from Strangeways dealt, is worth his weight in gold. When the gentleman from Strangeways made it known to Canky that he had taken on another client, and that demand was like to increase, Canky did what all sensible men of business do, he expanded. With Scrat`s agreement, they brought in first Bill Nimmy, then Ned Small and Sam Forcher, all of whom were hardened enough, and conscience-stripped enough, and most of all, greedy enough to be trustworthy.

But this was still in the future.

The second trip, which brought a fourteen year old maiden, taken by the consumption, to the Irwell basin, and to the safekeeping of the gentleman from Strangeways, left Canky and Scrat once again in the tavern on Old Mill Gate. This time, however, meeting up with a couple of sisters who were also in trade, they weren`t so quick to set one foot in front of another on the road back to Middleton.

When Canky`s first wife died some fuss was made during the church service because she was the wife and help-meet of one of the church`s own servants, the sexton – for so he was by now - Oliver Canky. It was a great shame, people said, that Canky had had to oversee the digging of his own wife`s grave, but such was the nature of life, of death, and of everything, and so it must be, Amen.

"We`ve got a commission," Canky told Scrat, on the night of his wife`s interment.

"Surely not your own wife!"

"Why not? She served little purpose else whilst she lived, why shouldn`t she serve the purpose of science now she`s dead?"

"But I saw you heaping the clay onto her coffin. I stood there and watched you do it. Surely, you`re not going to dig it all out again."

Canky looked at him with a restrained smile.

"I filled the coffin with a few bags of cinders and a bit of loam to make up the weight. She`s lying in the bedroom still. This`ll be an easy one. And then I`ll have my bedroom back to myself."

Chapter 29

"You should come to Norfolk, mother," said William Harbord, the second Lord Suffield, a title he had assumed after his father's death the previous year.

"Why didn't Caroline come with you?" asked Lady Anne, sharply.

"She's been a little unwell," said William, somewhat disingenuously, for though Lady Caroline was generally and perpetually in the grip of some minor ailment or other, there had actually been no genuine reason why she shouldn't accompany him to Lancashire had she wished to do so. The truth was that she didn't wish to do so. "Did she not mention it in her letters?"

"Probably," said Lady Anne, who had little patience with Caroline's tiny lady-like handwriting, with its loops and curls, and seldom got beyond the salutation and the first two sentences.

"She insisted that I should bring you to Norfolk."

There was some truth in this. Caroline, distressed and a little guilty at the number of letters her husband received from his mother, accusing him of neglect, both of herself and of the Middleton estates, had urged him to make this journey.

"Do try to persuade her to come to Gunton, William," she sighed, helplessly. "Why on earth she stays in that terrible place unless merely to provoke us, heaven only knows!"

To Caroline, of course, the sense that Middleton was a forlorn, alien and inhospitable place, was genuine. Even on her first visit, nearly twenty years before, when, recently a bride, she was eager to please and to be pleased, the dampness and rain had so depressed her spirits that there was no consoling her. Their visits since had been few and far between.

His own feelings were more mixed. To a child, one place is much the same as another, and with his mother and father and his younger brother, Edward, coming to Middleton once or twice a year, to see grand-mama, had been in the nature of a holiday. In fine weather – and he did remember some – there was the lake and a rowing boat, the river and a fishing-line, the park with its trees to climb. In wet weather, there was a long corridor, very suitable for practising cricket, and indeed, there were still marks on the wainscot where it had been struck by doughty blows from the leather orb. Even now, forty years later, when he found himself on that corridor, he could seldom resist the temptation to rehearse a stroke or practise a run-up and delivery.

For most of his adult life, however, travelling to Middleton had become a chore, and, as on the present occasion, he spent most of the time there wondering how soon he could decently get away from it.

"Why don`t you come down to Norfolk?" he repeated. "It`s so dreary here."

"To you. Not to me."

William sighed. His mother`s preference for Middleton had become legend in the family but he was sure it hadn`t always been so. In his very earliest of memories of her, she was a fashionable young woman who loved the pleasure of the theatre, of the assembly rooms, and of society – the pleasures, in other words, of London. This later partisanship for the place of her birth was, he concluded, a matter of stubbornness. Stubbornness, the weapon which an old woman has when all other weapons have failed. Still, she had to be humoured.

"Not so much dreary," he said, "that isn`t quite what I meant. What I`m saying is that it`s now getting on towards October, and you know how much healthier the Norfolk air is through the winter months."

This, it seemed, had as little effect as his other persuasive gambits. It was a great pity, he often reflected, that his marriage to Caroline hadn't been blessed with children; had his mother had grandchildren to fuss over, it might have been a different story, but as Caroline was now 44, it was unlikely that any surprises could be looked to from that quarter.

"There are so many more people for you to see at Gunton, chère maman," he said, vainly trying to soften her with a French endearment.

His preferred picture of her was that of a contented and serene gentle-lady, drinking tea, visiting, being visited, exchanging gossip and tittle-tattle with other gentle-ladies. If she would only fit in with that picture, he wouldn't have to worry about her so much. In fact, he would hardly have to think about her at all.

"There are plenty of people to see here," she replied.

"Who? Give me an example."

"Mrs Canky."

"Mrs Canky!" he scoffed. "Mrs Canky! And who, pray tell, is Mrs Canky?"

"She's a very interesting woman," said Lady Mary, recalling the very amusing account Mrs Canky had given her only the day before, of the science of progeniture as propounded by her husband, the sexton. "I enjoy her company a great deal."

"But who is she?"

"A seamstress."

"A seamstress! Oh, for heaven's sake, mother, try to be serious. When was the last time you visited, or were visited by, anyone of decent rank?"

"I don't want to be visited by anyone of rank. The state you and your father have let this hall lapse into, it's no longer a fit place to entertain people in, anyway."

"Now you know that's not true," said William, realising, with regret, that she had finessed him into talking about that other fixed idea of hers, that Middleton Hall should be restored to a grandeur which it had probably never had anyway. It was something with which, in his later years, his father had been

119

driven nearly to distraction. "But, I promise you, if you`ll come to Norfolk for the winter, I`ll get Brough to send one of his surveyors up here, and we`ll see what can be done. How`s that?"

She did not answer directly but he sensed, from her demeanour, that she was, in part at least, appeased. It occurred to him to think, there being little else now to be gained from prolonging the conversation further, that he might repair to the long corridor and rehearse a few strokes; even better, if one of the stable lads was on hand, to teach him the rudiments and play a few overs.

"Mr Gregge paid me a visit, since you ask."

"Hopwood?"

"Yes. He brought someone. Lord Byron. They came to pay me their respects."

"Good. I hope you received them properly."

"There`s an invitation on my escritoire," she added.

"An invitation."

"They`re having a soiree in honour of their visitor."

"Byron?"

"You`ve heard of him?"

William had heard something of Byron, but not much that he cared to remember. An impecunious upstart aristocrat who had inherited some worthless titles, had some unsightly deformity of the leg and an enormously fat mother, and who had put out a volume of puerile love poems and one of scurrilous satire.

"A little. Are you going to go?"

"No."

"Why not?"

"Because that hideous man, Ezekiel Barton and his tribe will be there."

"He`s not a hideous man, mother, he`s an industrialist, a man of the times. You know how much father admired Mr Barton."

"The more fool him."

William knew that to argue this one was to back a horse that wouldn't run, so he did not pursue it. Nevertheless, he made a point of going to the escritoire to look at the invitation. Mrs Gregge Hopwood, he recalled, was a rather fine young woman, and had two sisters, equally attractive. Besides, it would be no bad thing to have a chance to talk to Barton, for the fact was that a few more factories like his would certainly boost the revenue gained from rents on the estate, which, if they weren't going to do the thing unmentionable to his mother, and impossible during her life-time, that is, sell it off altogether, lock, stock and barrel, might be crucial.

"It would be churlish to reject the invitation outright, or even worse, to ignore it," he said to his mother at dinner. "If you won't go, I will."

"Very well," said Lady Mary, brought back from an elaborate detour of thought whereby she had been wondering if William and Caroline might have profited, at one time, from the scientific approach which had been described to her by Mrs Canky. "If you have a word with Howarth he'll make sure the carriage is ready."

Chapter 30

Lucy Brindle was not only thirsty, she was bored. A flatness lay across her nerves and spirit like a dull insipid mist. Mima and the other members of the household, thinking that she was simply absorbing the peace and tranquillity required to restore her spirits fully, did not question the torpid state in which she sat, in a corner of the kitchen, other than to smile and ask if there might be anything she wanted.

Kindness itself.

Only Simon looked at her curiously, seeming to peer at least some way down into those murky deeper currents and see something else besides the reflection of the sky.

"Is there anything you`d like, Lucy?" asked Mima, passing through the kitchen.

"No, I`m quite settled, thank you."

They exchanged a little smile. The transaction was done.

Was there anything she`d like?

Yes.

She`d like to be in a tavern in Church Street or Mill Gate, Withy Grove or Hanging Ditch having some raucous banter with the other girls.

She`d like to be having a bit of an ogle with some eager gallant by the bar who looked keen to part with his money, and who`d send a drink over as a prelude to something else.

She missed the night and the business of the night.

She even missed Skinner and if she missed Skinner there had to be something badly wrong.

She put her hand to her cheek where the bruise had been. That was Skinner`s work, and it was that which had brought her to Middleton on the whim of finding Scrat. It was just for a lark, no more than that, and she`d left plenty of hints for

Skinner to come and find her if he wanted to. Come to think of it, he probably had, knowing Skinner, though he would have had no way of knowing she was here, got up in clean linen, with a plain calico skirt and a white cotton blouse and mop-cat, sitting like a study of patience and virtue.

He wasn`t all bad, when it came down to it, was Skinner. He was easy to tease and taunt, though you had to mind the back of his hand when his temper was up. But he did his best to mind her, and though, as some of the girls said, he was soft as pig shit when it came to a proper fight, his size and brawn were usually enough to put anyone off who was trying any funny business. He was a bit like a dog, really – he had a nasty snarl, but if you threw him a stick he`d come bounding back with it, wanting you to throw it for him again.

"Anything you`d like, Lucy?"

"No, thank you."

And then another exchange of mild and well-intentioned smiles.

No thank you.

Unless you`d like to bring me a mug of ale to dampen down this dry thirst...

Unless you`d like to follow it with half a dozen gin swizzles to bring the world to what it ought to be, a place of uproarious mirth and jollity...

Unless you`d like to treat me, when all else is done, to a brandy...

No rubbish, mind you!

A fine brandy, a Cognac, a Bonaparte.

A bottle of Scrat`s Bonaparte would do very nicely, thank you very much.

Scrat, she reflected, the above list vanishing like meats at a Harpy`s banquet, was to blame for all this.

Scrat with his eager dick, and his come-to-see-me Lucy, and his house on the hill, and his keys and his padlocks, and his finest Bonaparte brandy, and his cellars.

And his cellars.

If it hadn`t been for what she`d suddenly turned to see, in the clammy coldness of Scrat`s bottom-most cellar, under the uncertain flickering of a candle guttering with wax, she would certainly have toddled straight back to Manchester, with two half-crowns for her troubles, and a couple of bottles of Bonaparte safely hidden away in her bag. She certainly wouldn`t have been found by Mima Bamford, the worse for one of those bottles, in the Middleton Shambles.

Scrat, she reckoned, owed her something.

And as they closed their eyes to say grace, and as they broke bread over the wholesome soup of carrot and mutton and barley which Mima had prepared, Lucy Brindle`s thoughts were turning to a question so obvious that it was a marvel she hadn`t thought of it before.

Owd Scrat had a secret. And owd Scrat, to judge from appearances, had some money.

The question was, how much of that money was that secret worth?

Whilst the Bamfords were thus at prayer, their eyes closed in earnest devotion, her eyes were open and turning towards Simon, she saw that his were open, too, and that they were looking directly into hers.

Chapter 31

S imon had been called through into the house to run an errand.

"There`s a package here to be delivered to Mrs Gregge at Hopwood," said Mima. "Some lace handkerchiefs. Sam`ll be going up to Manchester with the bulk on Thursday, but this is a separate order, and can be delivered directly."

Simon nodded, seeming moody, though in fact, there was nothing he liked better than to have a decent long errand that took him out of the way for a bit.

"I could go with him," piped up Lucy, suddenly, from her chair in the corner.

Both Mima and Simon looked towards her.

"I think I`m feeling well enough to go out now."

"I`m sure some air would do you good, Lucy, but it`s such a way."

"I know the way to Hopwood so well from when I was a girl, and loved it so much then, I`m sure it would be a tonic to my spirits to see it again."

Mima looked to Simon, to see if there were any sign of resentment at the prospect of being thus encumbered. His cheek was slightly flushed with pink, though whether from embarrassment or pleasure, she couldn`t tell.

"I hope he`s not going sweet on her," said Mima to Sam, as they sat working at their looms after the couple had set out.

"It might be no bad thing," said Sam. "He shows little enough interest in the girls of his own age."

"But think who she is, Sam, and she must be eight years his senior, too."

"Unrequited love is the stuff of poetry," replied Sam, airily. "A moderate infatuation for an older woman is no bad thing. It informs the sentiments and teaches the emotions to flow."

"Oh yes? And who was it informed your sentiments and taught your emotions to flow?"

"Oh, there were many of them, Mima," said Sam, dodging to avoid the bobbin which had been playfully thrown in his direction, "before I was led to understand where my heart truly lay."

"Oh, well spoken!" she said, in a tone of mock satire. "You know which side your bread`s buttered on, don`t you!"

By now he had crossed the room, and seizing her two small fists in his palms, was kissing her nose.

"Get away with you, you daft ha`p`orth," she said. "Anyone`d think there was no work to do in this house."

"Kiss me, then."

"No, let go of my hands."

"Kiss me and I`ll let go of your hands."

"No."

"Obey thy husband, woman."

"Honour thy wife, husband."

"I do."

"All right, then, just to keep the peace."

And with that she kissed him on the cheek, and then he clasped her in his arms for a moment with all the affection of a contented husband.

Meantime, Simon and his companion had passed Hollin Lane, on the way out of Middleton, and were nearing Stanycliffe. If there had been any doubts in Simon`s mind about Lucy`s fitness for the walk, they were now dispelled, for she kept up with him, pace for pace, and stride for stride, without showing any sign of fatigue.

"It`s quickest if we slip down through the clough," said Simon, "but if you`d prefer it we can keep on the lane as far as Slattocks and then turn into the Hall`s driveway."

"Let`s go through the clough, then," said Lucy. "We used to play there by the river when I was little. I want to see if it`s just as I remember it."

"Right, then," said Simon, leading the way over a stile and then following the narrow pathway down towards the little bridge over the Whit Brook. The canopy of high trees, their colour now changing, as September gave way to October, from gold to red, gave the clough a sheltered tranquil feel, still, apart from the constant babbling of the brook. There was enough sun, slanting through the trees to lift the shadowy gloom with patches of dappled light, but there was a scent of damp moss and toadstools, enough to give a potent hint of autumn's decay.

After fifteen minutes' walk, delaying here and there, at Lucy's request, to stand and listen to the brook or to watch for a hare which she had caught in the corner of her eye dashing through the bracken, they came to the pool where, not much more than a week before, Edward Gregge Hopwood's aristocratic guest had bathed in the morning sunlight.

"I'll wait here," said Lucy.

"Don't you want to come in and see? They take you into the drawing room to open the packet and sometimes they give you a cake or a sweetmeat."

Lucy shook her head. "I'd rather not. Mrs Gregge knew me once, and I don't want to be stared at."

"All right. I'll be as sharp as I can be. Don't go wandering off."

"I won't."

He set off at a canter, and Lucy, finding a dry flat stone shelf at the edge of the brook, sat down, took off her shoes, pulled up her skirts and dipped her feet in the water.

It was in this position - and in complete privacy, as she thought - that she was still sitting, when the trot of a pony on the driveway to the hall, brought its rider to the bridge immediately above. The rider, David Barton, sent by his father to pay his respects to Lord Byron and to accept the kind invitation of Mr and Mrs Gregge Hopwood to their forthcoming soiree, was immediately distracted by the sight he saw below. Tying his horse to a gate, he made his way down.

"Well, now, fair maid, I thought to have come across such a pretty picture only in the realms of poetry."

Lucy looked up and, nothing dismayed, calculated how much she might earn from continuing to let the popinjay indulge his fantasy. A guinea, she reckoned, maybe two, and she might have been game for it, too, had she not had other matters in hand.

"I`m waiting for my sweetheart," she said.

"I see no sign of him. Allow me to fill in the time between."

"And what, pray, are you going to fill it with, sir?"

David Barton, smiling, and acknowledging her to be shrewder than he might have reckoned, nevertheless took up the banter.

"I warrant I`ve something that would fill it very adequately."

"But would it last until my sweetheart returned?"

"That I can`t say, as it would depend on him. For my own part, I think I may be relied on to tarry a decent while."

"And you have already fulfilled your promise," said Lucy, "for here he comes already."

Looking up, David Barton saw, coming over the stile and towards them, the lad who he vaguely recognised as belonging to the Bamford household.

"Pity," he said. "I doubt if you`ll get much joy there."

"He`s very devoted to me," said Lucy, archly.

"The more fool him," said David Barton, putting on his dry satirical expression, and turning to go.

"What did he want?" asked Simon.

"Lost his way and needed direction," said Lucy.

Puzzled, Simon turned his head to see David Barton now remounting his horse, and then turned back. "Sorry," he said, suddenly noticing that Lucy`s skirts were drawn back over her knees.

"Don`t mind me," she said, seeing his reaction. "I`m just bathing my feet. You can look the other way if you`re shamed."

"I`m not shamed," he said, shrugging.

"Well, then, sit down for a minute. I've waited enough for you, now you can wait for me."

Obediently, Simon sat down. "I couldn't get away," he said, managing for a moment to take his eye off Lucy's shapely knee. "They kept asking me stuff. Well, he did, anyway."

"Who's *he*, Squire Hopwood?"

"No, his visitor. Some toff. Lord Somebody or other. Not from round here. I was telling the mistress what Mrs Bamford told me to tell her, you know, about the lace-work and that, and he didn't take his eyes off me all the time."

"Maybe he's a bit of a queer one. Or maybe not. You know you have a bit of a look of a girl about you. Maybe he was looking at you because he curious."

"Anyway, then I'd finished and I was ready to come away and this Lord so-and-so, gets up and walks over, with this funny limp he has, and he starts asking me about who my master is, and where we live, and all sorts of stuff. I thought I was going to be there all day!"

"Well, you're away now, so there's no harm done."

"I brought you this," he said, producing an orange and handing it to her, and feeling, as she accepted it, that he might just sneak a look at both knees together.

"I'll peel it, and we'll share it," she said, setting her nail into the skin of the orange and quickly working it off. Then, segment by segment, with the juice running over her fingers, she handed one to him, and then popped the next one into her own mouth, until it was finished. Then she dipped her fingers into the stream, dried them on the grass, and likewise her feet, and the put her shoes back on.

"Help me up," she said, offering the tips of her fingers, which he took, and then they began to make their way back through the clough.

They had just reached the midway point when Lucy stopped and drew him aside.

"What is it?" he asked, wondering if she had seen another hare starting, or some other distraction.

"I want to ask you to do something for me, Simon. A favour. Will you?"

"It depends what it is. If it`s in my power, I mean. How can I know?"

"It`s simple. I want you to take a message for me, to someone in Manchester."

"How can I get to Manchester? I`ve never been there in my life."

"Sam`s going to Manchester on Thursday. Mima said so. If you ask him, he`ll take you."

"What if he doesn`t?"

"He will. But if he doesn`t, then you`ll have tried, anyway, won`t you, and I`ll be equally grateful."

"All right, then, I`ll try."

Lucy produced a note of paper, folded over, and tied with a little bit of ribbon.

"Go to the Black Boy, it`s a tavern on Mill Gate, you`ll find it easily, and say you`ve got a message for a man called Skinner. They`ll know who it is. He`ll most likely be there himself, but if he`s not, say it can be entrusted to a lady called Nan. Have you got that. Either Skinner or Nan, no-one else."

"Right."

Then, at the point of handing it to him, she pulled it back.

"How do I know you won`t open it?"

"I won`t, I promise."

"How do I know that curiosity won`t get the better of you and make you break your promise?"

Simon seemed to have no ready-made answer for this, but Lucy did. She looked around, and then, seeming almost by accident to trip and fall against him, she slipped he hand into his breeches. The lad was obviously shocked but nevertheless came quickly to an erection, which Lucy attended to in the caressing way she knew all too well.

"If you deliver my message, and don`t open the seal, I`ll finish this off for you, I promise, when you get back. More, if you wish it."

"Won`t you finish it now?"

"All right, then," she said, feinting to do so for a full twenty seconds before stopping suddenly.

"What is it?" he said, in some anguish.

"Not here, someone`ll come by and see us for sure and then how will it stand, if word gets back?"

She took his hand and put it under her blouse, directly onto her breast.

"There," she said, "that`s in earnest of what I promise you, if you do what I ask."

For a moment, she nuzzled softly against him. "We must find a more shadowy place for this," she said. "And we will. When you get back from Manchester."

Chapter 32

"It's a great pity we aren't to have any dancing," said Millie Barton, Ezekiel Barton's elder daughter, to Eleanor, sister of Cecilia Gregge Hopwood. "It becomes tedious when all people do is sit and talk. Some dancing would be excellent on an occasion such as this."

Eleanor leaned towards her, confidentially, and whispered behind her fan. Millie's eye immediately sought out Lord Byron and travelled downwards towards his leg.

"Oh, I see," she muttered quietly.

Lord Byron was, at that moment, in conversation with William, Lord Suffield. [Two lords together! as Cecilia remarked to her husband] William was familiar with a number of the diplomats and expatriates Byron had encountered on his travels in Portugal, Greece, Turkey and Albania, and was able to offer some anecdotes about their eccentricities and foibles which he found amusing himself, though Byron maintained a polite reticence.

"Do you hunt, Byron?" asked Lord Suffield.

"I ride," said Byron. "Not well, but I ride. I don't hunt."

"Nor me. Can't really see the point. Cricket's my game. Did you ever see any cricket, at Harrow?"

"I played for the Harrow eleven against Eton, in 1803."

"Good lord!" said Suffield. "Did you really?"

"I scored eleven runs in the first innings, and seven in the second," said Byron, and then, noting the almost imperceptible glance of Lord Suffield towards his leg, added, "I employed a runner."

"Well, good heavens, a man after my own heart!"

"We lost rather heavily, as I recall," said Byron, "but nonetheless I recall the occasion with great nostalgia, and just a little pride."

"Let me tell you something, Byron, there`s a corridor at Middleton Hall most apt..."

"They seem to be getting on well," said Cecilia.

"Yes," said Robert, pleased that so far things seemed to be going smoothly, though thinking privately how very nice it would be, after his friend`s departure, when things got back to normal.

"But we mustn`t let Lord Suffield dominate our guest," Cecilia added. "There are others, I`m sure, who would like to share him."

"I would banish dancing altogether, should my husband wish it," said Cecilia`s younger sister.

"Eleanor, I do believe you`ve fallen in love with him!"

"Can I tell you something?" said Eleanor, flushing. "You know I told you about his poem to the Maid of Athens?"

"I think I remember..."

"*Maid of Athens, `ere we part,*

Give, oh give me back my heart."

"Oh, yes, I do remember."

"Well, in the courtyard, yesterday, I happened to pass him by as he was coming back from the river, and he actually said to me *Maid of Hopwood, `ere I part...*"

"He didn`t!"

"He did."

"And did he say the rest."

"No, he didn`t say the rest. But the intention was there. How else was I to take it?"

"I can`t answer that, but it would have been nice if he`d said the rest."

"Yes, it would," Eleanor conceded, with a sigh.

A short time later, in the sonorous but slightly nasal voice which he reserved for such occasions, Burley requested the Lords, Ladies and Gentlemen to proceed to the dining room where a cold standing supper awaited them.

"I`m glad to see you eating something besides your vinegar and water, Lord Byron," said Mary Lovejoy.

"One of the advantages of this kind of supper," he replied, "is that one is not forced to sit and be served until the plate begs mercy and then be studied by all around until it is empty again."

"The other advantage, of course, is that one is not forced to sit for an hour in the same immediate and possibly tedious company."

"How wicked of you to say so," said Byron, catching a satirical glint in Mary Lovejoy`s eye which he appeared to relish.

"I suppose, to be true to my own adage, I ought now to move on to converse with someone else. But here comes one," she added, seeing the approach of Lord Suffield, "who I suspect will rob me of the opportunity of being rude to you."

"I will make it my highest priority to create another such opportunity," said Byron.

"How kind of you. And you may be sure that I will take it!"

"Byron!" said Lord Suffield. "Have you met Barton? Ezekiel Barton, our Middleton industrialist."

The introductions were completed with expressions of polite admiration, each for the other`s achievements.

"In Nottingham, I`m told," said Byron, "there is a deal of consternation amongst the stocking weavers at the introduction of the new wide-frames which they believe threaten their livelihoods."

"It is a problem I`m well aware of," said Ezekiel Barton.

"We`re expecting a visit from Captain Ludd any day," said a young man, joining the group without introduction, though Byron recognised him as the fellow who had been received at the hall the previous day, a short time after the appearance of the stunningly beautiful boy who had arrived bringing finished silk work.

"My son, James," said Ezekiel Barton.

134

"What's that you say?" said Lord Suffield.

"I said we're expecting a visit from Captain Ludd," the youth repeated.

"Don't make light of it, James," said his father. "It's not a joke."

"Oh, I don't know..."

"There's a bill to be presented to parliament, Byron," said Lord Suffield. "You can join me supporting it in the House of Lords."

"I've only been to the House once," said Byron. "I've yet to make my maiden speech."

"No speeches necessary. It makes frame-breaking a capital offence. Straightforward and simple. All it needs is your support."

"A capital offence?"

"I'm not altogether sure that I could agree with that," said Ezekiel Barton.

"Oh, don't be coy, father. Off with their heads! That's what I say!"

"What I say is this," said Ezekiel Barton, ignoring his son's frivolity. "It is obstructions to trade, caused by the turmoil of war, and by misgovernment, that cause men to fear the loss of livelihood, not machines. Machinery brings the capacity to expand trade and bring prosperity to all."

"Quite right," said Lord Suffield, "and that's precisely why this bill has to go through. Deterrence, that's the word. And if you're worried about any assault on your premises, Barton, take my advice and get the militia to take up some billets in the town. That'll send the right messages out."

"I'm sure it won't come to that."

"Don't be complacent, Barton. Prepare for the worst and then you're ready for it. And if it doesn't come to it, well, you're none the worse."

"Come and meet my sister," said the young man, drawing Byron away, "she's dying to meet a famous poet."

"I can lay claim to neither of those titles."

"Well, come and meet her anyway. Once they get talking about trade there`s no stopping them, and it`s pretty dry stuff, too, let me tell you. Here we are. Lord Byron, meet my sister, Millie."

"Enchanted," said Byron, taking the young woman`s hand and raising it to her lips.

"I expect you know Eleanor already, but you`d best kiss her fingers, too, or they`ll be at each other like cats."

"David!" said Millie.

The young man laughed, pleased with himself.

At this point, Burley cleared his throat, and when the room became still, he announced that some entertainment, in the form of singing to the pianoforte, was presently to take place in the drawing room.

David Barton, still at Byron`s shoulder, sighed. "How tedious!" he said. "If it`s Cecilia Hopwood, I`ve heard better music from a strangled cat."

Cecilia sang with a high rather thin voice, but it was by no means as hard on the ears as the young man suggested, and her playing was good. Robert`s voice was a pleasing baritone, though he tended to forget the words of his song and to need prompting. They then performed a duet together, a playful love song, which was evidently their party-piece, and then, some eagerly, some with much persuasion, others came forward to offer a contribution.

"Do you sing, Byron?" said David.

"I shall not sing tonight."

"Nor me. I prefer a song in a tavern, to be quite honest. A good rousing chorus, with the cans clinking and the ale flowing. That`s my idea of a good night out. Now, when Sam Bamford gets up and does a turn in the tap room at the Boar`s Head, that`s what I call entertainment. None of this warbling!"

"Bamford," said Byron, thoughtfully. "That name was mentioned in connection with a parcel of silk that was delivered here, the other day."

"That's right. That's his lad, the queer looking one, his delivery boy."

"His son?"

"No, not his son. He has no father, well, I suppose he must have had one once, but some people say he was left by the fairies and it wouldn't surprise me, either!"

"So, this man Bamford sings at the Old Boar's Head?"

"Not so much sings. Recites. He's a poet. Like you I suppose, really, if you don't find comparison with a country rhymester insulting."

"Why should I?" said Byron. "But tell me more."

There was another round of polite applause as Mary Lovejoy completed a comic song about a shepherd, who distracted by love, lost a sheep from his herd each day for a week; and then, against all previous disclaimers, and as if inspired to cast off the impression of mild ennui with which he had presented himself beforehand, Lord Byron stepped forward to sing.

"How unpredictable he is," said Cecilia Hopwood.

"If I had my way," thought Mary Lovejoy, very privately, "I'd show him that an old bird can still fly."

"Two more days," thought Robert Gregge Hopwood, "three at the most..."

"Does he have many *amours*, do you think?" asked Millie Barton.

"I suspect many," said Eleanor, with another wistful sigh.

"But not married?"

"No, nor engaged, for anything that has been said or hinted at, but he is writing a very grand poem about his travels, and I believe that everything will be revealed there."

"I shall buy a copy and smuggle it into my bedroom!" said Millie Barton.

"Would your father object so much, do you think?"

"Probably not. But I should so much prefer to do it secretly."

The two girls sat together in silence for some moments, and then, together, drew such a sigh, and in such unison, that they seemed to be thinking the same thought.

Maid of Hopwood, `ere I part,
Give, oh, give me back my heart!

Chapter 33

O ne day, almost three years exactly after he had seen her married to Sir Robert Edgeworth at St Leonard's Church, Scrat caught a glimpse of his Dorothea once more. He was repairing some railings close to the bridge which formed one of the main entrances to Middleton Hall when, looking up at the sound of approaching horses, he saw a barouche, and as it passed by, he recognised its two passengers as Sir Robert and his wife.

As the carriage made its way round to the main entrance, Scrat took a short-cut through the orchard, and had reached a vantage point at the corner of the house in time to see them alight. No longer a girl, she seemed a picture of radiance and beauty, and as she stepped down from the carriage, aided by her husband's careful hand, it did not escape him that her form was that of a woman carrying a child.

"Curse him!" said Scrat, as he turned away into the concealment of the corner's return. "Curse him! He's taken what was mine." He closed his eyes, and squeezed them tight in bitter exasperation.

Over the next two days, drunk and sober, asleep and awake his feelings went through a volatile cascade of changing moods. To begin with he remembered the Dorothea who, in her plain dress and shawl, and with her hair flowing free down her back, had walked and run beside him along the lanes of Birch and Bowlee and Heaton Park those few years before.

Hand in hand, he recalled. He could look at his own palm now and recreate in his mind the exact sensation of hers resting against it. It reminded him of all the lofty aspirations he had felt then, not worldly or material ambitions, but aspirations of the spirit, poetic and sublime.

"What are you moping for?" asked Canky.

"Nothing."

"Sup up then and find your purse!"

His next shift of mood was to return to the cursing vein. Damn him to the very roots of his silver peruke; let him be strangled by his own silk neck-tie; may he be cursed with the scabies and the dropsy, the powdered popinjay, and then we`ll see what a pretty fellow he is, with the rheum dripping from his eyes and the pus oozing from his red-hot pimples!

One midnight, blind drunk, he was to be heard ranting and railing incoherently in the middle of the Warren, a bottle in his hand, and stumbling here, there and everywhere.

"Who on earth can that be, at this time of night?" said Jenny Canky.

"Shut up," said Canky. "I`m trying to concentrate. And so should you be."

"I don`t see how I can concentrate with that fyerin` racket going on."

"Don`t then, but don`t stop me, for God`s sake, not at this pass!"

"It`s more than human that noise is," continued Mrs Canky.

"It`s the noise of a drunken madman," said Canky, knowing full well that it was Scrat carrying on out there. "And if you don`t stop yours, I`ll put a pillow over your face!"

The next day, Scrat was consumed with melancholy, not just an ordinary sad melancholy, nor even a sickly hang-overish melancholy; it was a melancholy shot through with guilt and remorse and self-reproach.

He considered the picture of Melissa, so graceful, so beautiful, so pure of soul; and then he considered the condition of his own soul. Dear God, how far had he fallen since those days when his soul had been touched by love? His soul was now blackened and charred as if it had been hung in the most dense and most acrid smoker.

And he blamed Canky for that. It was Canky who`d got him into this filthy charnel-house business; it was Canky who`d introduced him, as if to Mephistopheles, to the shadowy friend from Strangeways; it was Canky who`d taught him the brusque etiquette of the dark alleyway, with Doll, or Meg, or Nan, or Lizzie or Nell. It was all Canky's doing.

"You nearly put me off my game last night with your midnight caterwauling," said Canky, in the Church Tavern, later that day. "My missus thought it was the horseman from hell."

"Maybe it was," said Scrat, his eyes cast downwards in the direction of his ale, still melancholy but by this stage a little more philosophical. "Maybe it was."

"Come on, then, what is it? I can`t stand this any longer. Tell me what`s brought all this on."

Reluctant at first to take into his confidence the man who, just a few short hours ago, he had considered his second most loathsome enemy after Sir Robert Edgeworth, Scrat, at last, after a few more, let it slip.

"And you`re letting yourself get worked up into a lather over that!" said Canky, in mere disbelief. "I thought it must be something more substantial than that."

"That`s because you`re a man of no feeling," said Scrat.

"Well, you might be right there," said Canky, not at all offended, "but before you slit your throat over them, you ought to consider what it is your feelings are about. Is it because you caught a glimpse of a pretty face? Course it is, but let me tell you something on that account. You see every day – at least I do – the fragrant loving wreaths and posies people leave on the graves of their dearly departed; now, in two days, maybe three, depending on the weather, you`ll see those flowers withered and dried out and not fit to be looked at. So it is with a woman`s face. And I`ll tell you something else, Scrat, there`s nothing more conducive to making a woman stout in the girth than giving birth to a child; and some it leaves flat-chested,

141

whilst others end up with dugs as heavy and gross as a cow`s udders, or even worse, somewhere in between, like empty flaps made out of parchment. You should consider all this before you sacrifice yourself on the altar of Dotty Edgeworth`s beauty. I tell you man, give it a year or two and you`ll be thanking Sir Robert for taking her off your hands, you`ll be running up to him and shaking him by the hand, and telling him he did you the best turn one man can do for another. So get your purse out, and let`s have another so that we can drink a toast to the brave Sir Robert!"

Forced, in spite of himself to grin, Scrat did as Canky bade him, and before the night was out, he felt himself shedding his melancholy as a snake sheds its skin. And when, not many days later, a further trip to the meeting place of the Irk and the Irwell was in the offing, Scrat found himself quite ready to make one of the company.

It was four months later that the news began to spread that Lady Edgeworth had died in childbirth.

Scrat heard it from one of the prattling under-maids at the hall.

"Dorothea," said Scrat, instinctively.

"Dorothea," echoed the under-maid, mockingly. "Hark at him, with his Dorothea!"

"I knew her once," said Scrat, quietly.

"Course you did, Scrat. And I`m the Queen of Sheba!"

Not wanting to get into a petty altercation, he took himself off to a quiet spot in the gardens, on a bank overlooking the river where it had been diverted to feed the lake.

"Dorothea," he said again, looking at the letters of her name which his finger had traced in the sandy loam. He felt a curious sense of lightness. Death had cheated Sir Robert of her, just as life had cheated him of her. All was equal. It was over now. Finished. And none of the things which Canky, in his grotesque parody, had predicted, could happen to her now.

He stayed sober for three days, and then went to find Canky in the churchyard. He found him in a newly dug grave, the top of his head, and the work of his spade just visible.

"Is this for her?" he asked.

"I`d be lying to you if I said it wasn`t."

"It`s deep."

"It`s for three. Her. Him. The child eventually, I suppose, when it grows up and dies. You have to allow a couple of feet extra."

Canky climbed up out of the grave, and wiped his brow. "Quite a job that. Anyway, it`s done now. She`s going in tomorrow, so it`s a job well done."

Scrat peered down into the grave. Canky took a drink from his water bottle, poured some of it onto his rag, and wiped his brow again.

"I know this might be a sensitive topic with you, Scrat," he said, but I have to mention it anyway…"

"Mention what?"

"Ashes to ashes, dust to dust…"

"What do you mean, you have to mention that to me?"

"You know what. Our friend from Strangeways was hereabouts yesterday."

"And what?"

"Like I said, you know what."

Scrat shook his head, and put his hand on Canky`s arm. "No!" he said vehemently.

"All right," said Canky, feeling the pressure of Scrat`s hand.

"I must have a say in this," said Scrat.

"All right," said Canky, "you shall."

"I mean it, Canky!" Scrat repeated, in deadly earnest.

"All right, all right. You can have it your way, I`ve not promised him anything yet."

Scrat breathed out deeply and let go his grip on Canky`s arm.

"I don`t know what the fuss is, though," Canky went on, rubbing his arm as if the impression of Scrat`s clasped fingers was still there. "I mean, what use is she to anyone down there?"

Chapter 34

When they reached to top of Blackley Hill, just past Boggart Hole Clough, there was a sharp shower of rain, and they took shelter under some trees at the edge of a spinney. There was a suggestion that the group of weavers, meeting up in their usual haphazard fashion on the way to the 'bearing home', might retrace their steps to the White Lion in the village through which they'd passed ten minutes before, but it was early in the day for that.

Sam Bamford had been worried at first that Simon would not be able to keep up with the stiff pace that the weavers set, but so far, two and a half miles on, he was holding his own.

"He'll be able to help you with the load," said Mima, her usual self, full of enthusiasm. The initiative had come from Simon himself and she didn't want his self-esteem to be punctured by a refusal. Sam had not been, initially at least, so keen to oblige. The fact was that he rather enjoyed his day of independence, exchanging views in the forthright way the men had, without having to defer to the tender ears of women and children. But he acknowledged, at last, that this was a selfish motive, and Simon was old enough to get his first glimpse into the rough and tumble world of the working men.

"You will mind him up in Manchester, won't you, Sam?" said Mima, before they set out. "Don't let him get lost."

After ten minutes, the worst of the squall had passed over, and they set out again towards Harpurhey.

As usual, every man had a tale to tell.

"There was a family evicted in Rhodes last week," said Ned Lock, who was from that district, and who'd cut up through Alkrington Wood to join the others.

"What, weavers?"

145

"Aye, weavers. Bailiff said as how his rent had gone unpaid five weeks. `How can I pay the rent when there`s no work?` he said. `Go and work in yon factory`, says the bailiff. `I`d rather eat grass and horse-muck before I`d go there,` says he. `Well, happen it`ll come to it,` says the bailiff, and had them out, anyway. The lad didn`t think he`d do it, but he did. `I`ll be knocking on Squire Heaton`s door over this`, says he. `Who do you think sent me?" says the bailiff. Well, some of his lads with him were sniggering at this, but there weren`t many looking on who were laughing, I`ll tell you that. You know what they were thinking, it`s him this week, happen it`ll be me next week."

Another fellow, who for some reason was just called Snick, took up the tale of a lad from Royton who`d had to send his wife and weans out begging at the corner of the town. `Someone said, why doesn`t he come and beg himself instead of putting his wife to shame, but when they got back they found him dangling from a rafter on the end of his own rope, so that answered that question right enough.`

There were other tales of hardship and misery, some of them evidently coloured up for the benefit of the listeners, for nobody likes to tell a bland tale, but there was a pattern, sure enough.

"It`s the way the country`s run," said one. "They may sit round in parliament and think themselves good men, and so they may be, honest men who say their prayers and hope to get to heaven, but if they could see what havoc the laws they pass wreak on folks like us, they`d have something to put to their own consciences, by heck they would!"

"What I`ve heard," said Sam Bamford, who`d begun to do a little reading on the Radical movement which was gaining a reputation – or notoriety – "is that we should have marches and gatherings, demanding an annual parliament and getting rid of the rotten boroughs, so that all men are properly represented."

"A vote for every man," said another.

"I'm not sure of that," said Sam. "I mean it sounds all right, I'll give you that, but you have to think how it could be managed. If I've come to any conclusion, it's this: however bad things are, they'd be worse if things descended to chaos, and there are some people who'd have it so."

"That's what they say happened in Paris, twenty years ago, and then worse than before until Bonaparte came along, but now look what a pother he's brought on the world."

"Aye, and on us as bad as on anyone. It's war that smashes up the way the trade runs, it takes the work away, and then it puts up the price of bread so that folks have no choice but to starve."

"Talking of the military matters," chimed in another, "I heard it said by someone who works at Barton's that the Scotch Greys from Manchester have been invited to Middleton, and you know what for, don't you? Just to warn any folks who might be thinking of making cause with Ned Ludd what they might expect."

"Who's Ned Ludd?" said Simon, as they approached Shude Hill, on the outskirts of the town, and as the group began to disperse, each to his own putter-out.

"He's a man of violence," said Sam. "A man who believes that the way to go about things is to smash up the new frames."

"And is that not a good way, if people are starving?"

"No, it's not. Nothing will be achieved if it isn't achieved within the rule of law. But look, we're drawing near our place of business, now, and I think the best thing is if you stick close by me until we've done."

If he'd had a choice in the matter, this is exactly what Simon would have done. He had enjoyed the two hour walk, listening to the men, for there had been a fair amount of choice language, and a fair amount of joking and laughter amongst the grimmer tales, but the town of Manchester, which they now approached, and which was like nothing he had ever seen before, had a suitably intimidating effect.

However, he had not forgotten the note from Lucy which was clutched in his pocket, and the reason for his mission.

"I thought I might like to have a look at the market, and a bit of a walk round, while I'm here, is that all right?"

"I promised Mima I'd not let you get lost."

"I won't. I'll stay near here, and keep coming back so I don't lose my bearings."

"You see that place, just down that street on the other side of the stalls?"

"The church?"

"That's right. That's the Old Church. You can see the steeple from most directions. Keep it in your view, and always come back there. That's where I'll meet you, in the Old Church yard. And if you get lost, that's the place you ask for."

"Right."

"You can walk as far as the river, but don't cross over it, or you can easily lose your way, and you have to watch out for yourself on the outskirts of a town sometimes more than you do in the middle of it where there's a lot of people minding what's going on."

"Right," said Simon.

"You'll hear the church clock strike twelve in a minute or so. When it strikes two, make sure you're there to meet me. And if I'm a bit late, just wait for me there. Here's a shilling. You can get yourself a pie at one of the stalls, but don't go into any public houses, because there's all sorts of rum folk who fetch up in them during the day when honest folk are working."

With this, and a few more assurances from Simon, they parted company, and Simon found himself alone amidst the throng of people who, unlike him, seemed to know exactly what they were doing and exactly where they were going, and to be getting on with it at great speed and without a care in the world.

Chapter 35

Through the whole of supper, Simon was aware of Lucy`s eyes. They were looking towards him, not constantly – for that would draw the attention of others – but with an expectancy all the more startling for its intermittent nature.

"Tell me what happened!" her eyes were saying. "Give me a sign. A nod of the head, however slight, a shake of the head…"

She even went to the point, when she was sure no-one else was looking, of giving a nod herself and raising her brows as if to say, look, I`ve done the hard bit, now just give me a tiny affirmation.

After meeting up with Sam, in the Old Church yard, they had revisited the market, and Sam, saying he was feeling extravagant, had bought a small chicken, already plucked, to bring home to eat.

But despite this, the mood around the table was sombre. The work Sam had brought home was a poor fraction of what had been expected, just as the last load had been less than the month before. Slowly but surely it was getting worse.

"If we`re to have only one loom working, then," said Mima, as brightly as ever, "tomorrow, I`ll walk out to the White Moss and bring home some blackberries. It`s just the time of year, and there may even be some elderberries left by the banks of the river. Lucy can come with me, if she likes."

Simon caught Lucy`s look at this moment, distracted as it was from its own eager quest, to convey the utmost dismay at the prospect of going a-blackberrying.

"Let me do the washing up," said Lucy, when the meal was done. "Come and help me, Simon. Mima and Sam have things to talk about, I`m sure."

They carried the plates and cutlery through to the kitchen, and Lucy closed the door.

"Well?" she said, abruptly, standing directly in front of him.

"Well, what?" he replied, shrugging his shoulders and feigning ignorance to tease her.

"Never mind well, what! Did you see him?"

"I went to the Black Boy."

"Yes?"

"And he wasn`t there. I asked if there was someone called Nan, but they said she wasn`t there either. They said I might find Skinner at the Feathers, though."

"He doesn`t usually go in the Feathers till later on, but go on, if I`d thought of it I could have told you to look there if he wasn`t at the Black Boy. So, did you find him there?"

"It was a proper goose chase. There was a woman there said he`d called in at the Feathers on some business first thing..."

"That`d be Lizzy. Did she say her name was Lizzy?"

"She didn`t say what her name was."

"Tall, plump girl, pretty face but a crooked nose."

"Yes, it could have been."

"You didn`t give the note to her, did you?

"No."

"Good lad. That`d be Lizzy, and if he had business there, I know what kind of business it would have been, too, but never mind her, did she say where he`d gone?"

"She said she thought he might be at the Vine."

"Oh, no, not the Vine! She didn`t send you there, did she? I could have warned you if I`d thought on. I might have known that she`d take one look at you and send you to the Vine. And did they send you into the back room at the Vine?"

"They did."

"You poor thing."

"He wasn`t there."

"No, he wouldn`t be. So what did you do? I`m surprised you got out of there at all."

"In the end I went to the Black Boy again, only because it was on my way back to where I was to meet Sam, and it turned out that he`d been there all the time."

"There you are! I told you that`s where he`d be! And did you give him my note?"

"Yes."

"And did he read it?"

"Yes."

"And you didn`t break your promise and read it first, did you?" she said, suddenly grabbing him by the hair and bringing his face next to hers.

"No. Ouch, let go."

"Good boy," she said, now patting his cheek gently. "I`ll have to think of some nice reward for you."

"You`ve already promised me my reward," he reminded her.

"Course I have," she said. "But I mean another one, too. You can have two rewards, can`t you?"

On the whole, Simon wasn`t displeased with his day`s outing, and not just because the successful delivery of Lucy`s message was equated, in his mind, with the dark excitement of anticipating his promised reward. If he`d been bewildered and intimidated at first by the sights and sounds of the town, the jabbering of the hucksters, the swarms of people, the hustle and bustle, he had not been out of Sam Bamford`s company for long before he began to find his feet and to enjoy his adventure.

He soon found the Black Boy, and though it was true that they had sent him on a merry dance from there, for their sport, no doubt, he`d been intrigued by the little glimpses it afforded him of the world to which Lucy belonged. To begin with, in the Feathers, whilst he was waiting, he`d been approached by an old man in a tail-coat, with a dirty yellow waistcoat, blue knee breeches and grubby white hose, speckled with mud, who, claiming to be a maker of portraits, had offered him half a crown if he would go with him to his studio to have his likeness painted. The girl – the one Lucy had supposed to be Lizzy - had shooed the old man off with a few sharp words well chosen to mortify his ears, and had asked him what his business was. When he turned to see who it was addressing him, he saw not a crooked nose – though she might have had one – but a bosom so prominently displayed that its central declivity might have been a crevasse into which an unsuspecting victim might easily fall and be lost forever.

But her voice, once she had despatched the old man, was strangely soft and caressing. Sitting him down in a corner, she had asked him what his errand was with Skinner, and when he told her that he had a message for him from Lucy, her face had taken on first a sly look, and then a look of tender concern, and at that point she had put her hand, as if by some natural and innocent instinct prompted sympathy, onto his knee, where it caused a tingling sensation quite unrelated to its apparent purpose.

"Poor Lucy!" she said. "We`ve been so worried about her. It makes my heart beat faster just to hear her name spoken," and with this, she took his hand with her other hand, the one that was not on his knee, and pressed it against her breast. "Can you feel my heart beating?"

"I think so."

"It`s very fast, isn`t it?"

Simon nodded his head. "Quite fast."

"Mr Skinner was here, earlier today, on business. He`ll be so sorry he missed you. But if you`d care to leave poor Lucy`s message with me, there couldn`t be a safer way to be sure that he will receive it."

Not entirely unaware that he was in a situation of negotiation, Simon toyed with the idea of seeing what he might get for his side of the bargain, but in the end his loyalty to Lucy prevailed.

"She said I mustn`t give it to anyone else, but only to him directly."

His hand was released from the bosom. Hers withdrew from his thigh, along which it had encroached somewhat, back to his knee, and then departed entirely.

"Go to the Vine," she said, all interest now lost. "You`ll find what you`re looking for there."

The Vine, as he followed the directions he was given, was in an altogether more remote and more shabby district of the town, and he was reminded of what Sam had said, warning him about straying too far afield. But though the alleyways were narrow, and shadowy even now in the middle of the day, and though the buildings seemed dilapidated, when he at last found his way into the Vine, it seemed that there were plenty of well-dressed gentlemen there.

"I`m looking for Mr Skinner," he said to the pot-man.

"Through in the back room," said the pot-man, casually nodding his head in the direction of a corridor at the side of the bar. "If he`s looking for you that`s where he`ll be."

Taking this cryptic reply at its simplest face value, Simon followed the direction of the nod of the head, finding himself, after a moment entering a room with no windows but only candle-light, filled, not entirely but almost so, with people as young as himself. They were dressed, some as page-boys in neat silver periwigs and smart livery, and some as white maidens such as one saw when the parishes celebrated the May, but the strange thing was that look as he might, it was almost impossible to tell which of them were girls and which were boys.

He stood for some time, looking at the curious scene, and no-one seemed to mind that he was there. It was almost as if he had become invisible. And then someone came towards him, singling him out, and he felt his lips being lightly pressed, in a kiss, by other lips. Then the person turned and walked away. He wanted to call the person back, to reciprocate the gentle soft kiss, and to see who it was, page or maid, girl or boy who had caused such exquisite sensations, but the person was already lost in the crowd.

Then, in a sudden tumult of panic, thinking that Sam would be waiting for him, he ran out of the place, and, when he had found his way out of the maze of alleys, he heard the church clock striking one. There was still an hour to go. With Lucy`s note still clasped in his hand, he decided to try the Black Boy one more time.

Once she had got the information from him that she wanted, Lucy left Simon to finish the washing-up and retired to her own little bed-chamber on the second floor. The note had told Skinner to meet her at the stile, opposite the Boar`s Head, set back a little from the road under the shelter of some trees. She also told him about Scrat and having something on him, enough for him to get the gist that she might need his help if there was any rough-house about it.

So far so good.

Tomorrow night, for that was when she had told Skinner to meet her, she would be heading back to the Black Boy with what she intended to be a sizeable pay-off. She had no doubt that Scrat would keep his money secretly hidden away at the house – given everything else that he kept there in secret – and to judge from his store of wines and spirits it was likely to be a fair stash. Once she put the proposition to him, he would have no option but to part with some of it.

It was no more than she deserved. She still woke up in the middle of the night, shivering and sweating, and in all her dreams, she was setting her feet one after the other, down the rough-hewn steps that led to Scrat`s second cellar.

She remembered noticing that the air was growing cooler as she descended, and if the first cellar had the kind of stale musty atmosphere that you might expect in a place that never had any proper change of air, the odour that now came to her nose was peculiar and sharp, pungent with something of a chemical nature like camphor or vitriol.

Four steps. Five steps. She stopped, trying to peer beyond the yellow circle of her candle flame to what lay beyond. A clammy sweat had broken out on her brow. Go back, her inner voice told her, go back and get your bottle of Bonaparte, and skedaddle off in the morning mist, on the road back to Manchester.

She took another step, this one the last, she promised herself, and just as she was about to turn, something soft touched her cheek, and though she realised straight away that it was just a spider`s web, it was too late to prevent a scream of shock issuing from her throat. She froze, hearing the scream reverberating in the vault below, terrified at the sound she had herself made, for if anything was lurking there, unaware of her presence, it must surely know she was there now.

The stillness resumed, and as it did so, her nerves became calmer. Her mind was playing tricks with her. There was nothing there; it was just a store-house, no doubt, a glory hole for Scrat`s old bric-a-brac.

She took another two steps and then realised there were no more. She had reached the bottom. It appeared to be a narrow chamber, with brick walls and a low vaulted ceiling, just a little above her own head-height. The candle guttered for a moment, and during that moment a panic gripped her heart that it would go out and leave her in darkness. Carefully, she tipped away some of the pooled wax, and now the flame stood up taller, showing her that a few feet ahead, fixed into the wall, was a cabinet whose glass just caught the reflected glow of the candle.

Curiosity now moved her step forward to look into it, and what she saw at first startled her and then charmed her. It was a small dog, so life-like that, were it not so still, you would swear it was alive. A little dog, with one paw raised, and its head cocked slightly to one side as if begging for a tit-bit. Even

155

the eyes, though she realised they were just painted glass beads, seemed to have a plaintive expression.

And there was more. Much more. On a shelf, next to the cabinet were various rodents, similarly preserved, two field mice and a baby, as if all three had been taken from the nest, a lithe brown rat bearing its teeth at another rat, a weasel, a stoat, a ferret.

A little further on she came across birds, some of them mounted on perches, some of them suspended on wires as if in flight, a raven, a tiny sparrow, a greenfinch, a magpie, a beautiful kingfisher.

Next, in another cabinet was a stealthy fox, his head turned as if to trace a sound it had just heard, its tail resplendent. Next to it was a black cat with a high straight tail, and then a fighting dog, its teeth set in what you could imagine as a vicious snarl.

This menagerie, she realised, was Scrat`s handiwork. It had a strange sinister beauty that made you shiver, but still, somehow, you wanted to go on and see what else was there.

At the end of this gallery, the room formed the shape of a tee, with a cell each way, right and left. Holding her candle into the right hand cell, she saw a table with the tools of Scrat`s art set out, bottles of chemicals, knives, scalpels, wire, scissors. There was also, somewhat disgustingly, in a jar above, what seemed to be the pickled head of a pig, and in another, similarly pickled, a brood of tiny kittens, pressed together as if in the womb, the blind faces pushed bluntly against the side of the jar.

Feeling sick, and not wanting to see any more, she stepped back, and turned.

And it was then that the yellow light of the candle, revealed, lying on a bier of polished wood, her head lifted on a crimson cushion, and wearing the white lace smock in which she had been dressed for her grave, the partially preserved remains of Dorothea Edgeworth.

Chapter 36

"The Old Boar`s Head?" said Robert Gregge Hopwood, in response to Byron`s question. "It`s a coaching house. We passed it the other day; you see it from the church brow, down below, by the turnpike."

"Is it respectable?"

"It`s a tavern. The hunt calls there occasionally, I only know it from that. More respectable than some, I suppose. Rowdy at times I`m led to believe, but then I don`t suppose it would be a tavern if it wasn`t. Why do you ask?"

"Oh, no reason in particular. It was mentioned by someone the other night. I can`t remember who."

Robert Gregge Hopwood shrugged his shoulders complacently. The soiree, it was generally agreed, had been a success, and now that it was over, interest in the young aristocratic visitor had waned somewhat. Cecilia had gone to stay with a sick relative in Bury, taking Eleanor with her. "The girl`s moonstruck," she had confided in her husband. "It would be no bad thing if he were to make his departure before we get back."

"He keeps threatening to do so, my dear, but as yet..."

Of course, with Cecilia away, he might well spend more time with Byron on the pursuits he favoured when in an active state of mind – he enjoyed fencing practice, which, he asserted kept his weight down, he enjoyed going out with his pistols or a hunting gun, for target practice, and then of course there were his madcap schemes for riding out in the middle of the night - but he had no intention of doing so. What he intended to do was to see his gamekeeper, and his estate manager, and to plan a round of visits to his tenant farmers; and to have a glass of port after his dinner, and to smoke a pipe, thoughtfully, by the fireside, followed by a night-cap of brandy until the inclination of sleep came upon him: in other words, to settle himself back, as fully and as quickly as possible, into the comfortable habits of a country gentleman`s routine.

"Have you heard anything more from Hanson?"

"He was going to go back to Rochdale yesterday, but the note I received at breakfast today said he`d been delayed by a bilious attack. To be perfectly honest, I begin to wonder if it might not have been better to conduct the business by letters from the very start."

"You must be missing the bright life of London?" Robert suggested.

"Not a great deal," said Byron, flatly. "Not at all, in fact."

This was not quite what Robert Gregge Hopwood was hoping to hear; but he drew comfort from the fact that it was not at all uncommon, as far as his own knowledge of the 6th Lord went, for him to say one thing, and then to discover, a short time later, that he actually felt the opposite.

Chapter 37

Mima had gone to bed, not long after supper, complaining of a head-ache. She had insisted, however, that Sam should go out as planned to the Boar's Head, where, by popular request, he had been asked to do one of his turns,

"Go!" she said, "You'll enjoy it, and I shall have some peace."

Sam looked on with the doleful eyes he always did when anything was wrong with Mima.

"I'll be right as rain in the morning," she said, "so you can stop your fretting. Now, go! And mind you don't wake me when you come in."

"I'll be as quiet as a mouse," Sam promised.

"As clumsy as a bear, more like," she teased.

It was about half an hour after Sam's departure that Lucy, who had also gone for a lie-down, or so she said, appeared again, wearing her old crimson velveteen jacket and skirt, and her feathered bonnet.

"Come up nice, don't you think?" she said to Simon, gesturing to her outfit.

"Where are you going?" said Simon, suspiciously.

"Who says I'm going anywhere?"

"What are you dressed up like that for, if you're not going out?"

"I might just be dressing up to give myself a bit of pleasure and cheer myself up. Don't you think I look nice, Simon?" she said, posing so that the green glass beads and ring were shown to good effect.

"Yes," he said, begrudgingly, the note of suspicion still in his voice.

"Tell true," she said, making a slight pose of vanity for him. "Say it."

"I think you look lovely."

"Oh, you`re such a sweet one, Simon," she said, pinching his cheek. "You`re a charmer, a right one, too!"

"Where are you going?" he repeated.

"Nowhere. Just out for half an hour. I have to meet someone."

"The man I took the letter to?"

"Don`t ask so many questions!"

"Who is he?"

"Just an old friend. Just meeting for a chat, for old time`s sake."

"It`s more than that isn`t it?"

"I told you, stop asking questions, you`re only upsetting yourself."

"He looked a rough sort. What do you want to meet his sort for?"

"I can meet who I like."

"I`m going to tell Mima," he said, moving to the door. "I`ll wake her up and tell her."

"Oh yes?" she said, standing her ground, and putting her hands to her hips in an attitude. "Go on, then, do it."

Sensing that she had another card yet to play, he hesitated at the door.

"Go on, then," she said again. "Do it. What`s stopping you?"

"And what will you do?" he ventured, tentatively.

"What will I do?" she said, as if in abstract speculation. "Now let me think. Well, for one thing, I might tell her what you were up to the other day."

"What do you mean?"

"How you made me go down through the clough instead of by the proper road. How you forced me into the bushes and tried to have your way with me. I might start with that."

Simon was silent. He did not even utter a `but...`. It struck him with sudden deadly force that she would tell such a lie, and that even if they didn't believe her, he would be made to give his version of events, which would mean him lying, too.

"Don't look so worried, chuck. It needn't come to that. Now, move away from the door, and let me pass."

"I'm going to come with you."

"No, you're not," she said slipping by him and making towards the front door, where she turned. "If you set one foot after me, I'll tell the whole sorry tale, I will, and then it'll be your look-out, Simon, so think on."

She went out through the front door, leaving him in the hall, where, for a few moments, he stood, out-manoeuvred, and disconsolate. And then it struck him that in the game of bluff and counter-bluff, the advantage, now she had left the house, was on his side. But it wasn't just a game. His motives were strong and pure. He had never felt any love for a woman and thought that he never could, because of something in his own nature. Since the first time he'd seen Lucy, however, and a pitiful sight it was, he had felt such tenderness towards her that it was just like the pangs of love; and now, after being in Hopwood with her, seeing her bathing her feet in the stream, her shapely ankles and calf, and the soft white flesh of her thigh, and with what had happened soon afterwards, the thought of her going out to meet someone else, consumed him with jealousy.

A short time later, hearing his footsteps behind her, she turned on him. "I warned you, Simon. I'll tell on you. I'll tell them everything I've said I will, and more besides."

"Go on, then," he said. "Tell them. What do I care? They're not my parents. Everyone thinks I'm a queer fish, anyway, so why should I care what anyone says?"

"Oh, Simon," she said, gently. "You're not a queer fish at all. You're lovely, that's what you are. An angel. You're an angel."

She smiled and touched his cheek. "My angel, that's what you are."

"Then let me come with you and watch over you."

"I`m just meeting up with an old friend. I`ll be back soon. You go home and wait for me there."

She enclosed his face with her hands, and, drawing him forward, kissed his brow. "Go home and wait for me there," she repeated, in the most practical and reassuring of tones, and then she turned, and began to walk on.

"You`re not coming back, are you?" he called after her, in a voice that was almost a wail.

She walked on, ignoring him

"What have you got to make old Scrat cough up?" he called after her, his voice fraught with tears.

She stopped and turned, looking at him with murderous intent.

"You promised me you wouldn`t open it."

"I didn`t. It was him who opened it. He asked me who Scrat was, and then he said the rest to someone else."

She looked at him intently, and then, as if deciding to believe him, softened her tone. "It`s just a jest. Just a bit of fun. Now, you go back."

She walked on again.

"I kept your promise. You promised me something too…"

She stopped, and turned, walking back towards him. "You`ll have to get someone else to do it for you, Simon. Another girl – or a boy, I expect you`d enjoy that just as much."

She laughed and turned away again.

"He said something else," he now called after her. "He said he`d be damned if he went chasing after the likes of you again."

"What`s this, then?" came a man`s voice from the shadows behind them.

Simon`s first instinct was to think it was Skinner, the very man they were talking about, arriving just in time to complete the nightmare, but he realised straight away that it wasn`t a rough, cussed voice like that of the man he`s met in the Black Boy; quite the opposite: it was a well-spoken voice, an easy slightly mocking voice.

"Well, I may have to have you two arrested for a breach of the peace!" he mocked.

As the speaker emerged from the shadow, Simon recognised David, the son of Ezekiel Barton, who had accosted Lucy at the river in Hopwood.

Lucy was still looking at him with fierce, yet almost pitiful directness, as if questioning or challenging the malice of what he had said.

"Why don`t you trot along home, young fellow," said David Barton, who, already slightly tipsy, was on his way from the Church to the Boar`s Head, where, he`d heard, there was some fun going on. "You trot along home, and leave me to look after the damsel in distress."

Lucy looked sideways at him for a moment, then looked back to Simon, and then, spitting directly downwards, as if for the benefit of them both, turned sharply and walked away at a pace.

Chapter 38

The landlord of the Boar`s Head had brought his daughter, Meg, and his daughter-in-law, Susan in to help with the service, as he often did when he knew in advance that it was going to be a busy night. To speak the truth, they were good for business anyway because they were both feisty good-looking girls who could turn on the frolicsome eye, and nothing pleases a drinker more than to be served his ale or his porter by a wench with some spirit who didn`t mind a bit of banter and the occasional pinch on the backside.

It had been a good day for business all round, he reflected. The tap room was full and was like to remain so for a good two hours, and in addition he had some paying guests. An elderly lady, travelling to Carlisle with her daughter and grandchild had decided to break the journey when the infant became sick, and a gentleman traveller, who was also paying for his horse to be stabled, had not minded taking the garret room accessed by the outside staircase. The ladies had taken a light supper in their room; the gentleman had said that he would not eat: but to have three rooms let at once was no bad thing, it was all money in the till.

Sam Bamford was just beginning his second recitation of the night. It was an old favourite, the one about the doctor.

I sing of a doctor, a doctor I sing
God send such a doctor to every bad king;
For this is a quack of superlative skill –
If he cannot cure he can certainly kill.

There was a guffaw of laughter which rolled across the whole room. The landlord himself grinned broadly. The quack doctor – and God knows there were enough of them – was always good for a joke, but he sensed that it was what was coming next that they were really laughing at. That was the strange thing – they`d heard it before a dozen times, and yet somehow, the anticipation of what they already knew was almost funnier than hearing it for the first time.

God send such a doctor to Sawney the Russ,
God send such a doctor Frederick the Pruss,
To Ferdi and Francis, and Louis the lame,
There`s another besides – need I mention his name?

And there it was, right on cue, a huge wave of laughter, just as the landlord had predicted. There was nothing men liked better than being shoulder to shoulder with other men, with a tankard in their hand, and sharing laughter as if it was all cut from the same piece.

"Susan," he said to his daughter-in-law, "make your way over and tell him to pause for five minutes whilst folk have a chance to fill up their glasses. Meg, go and see that our young gentleman lodger is tended to."

The gentleman traveller had taken a seat alone in a private room reserved for paying guests, though with the door open it still commanded a view over the proceedings in the tap-room and the young gentleman, though his expression changed little, seemed interested enough to pass the time by watching the scene.

The landlord was now distracted by an influx of new customers who had made their way up from the Assheton Arms, having heard that there was a bit of a lark to be had just up the road.

"Welcome one, welcome all," said the landlord in jovial fashion. "Take a seat gentlemen – Meg, bring through more stools – and Meg will provide you with something to quench your thirsts."

"She can provide us with more than that, if she pleases, Will!"

"Aye! Aye!" said the landlord, allowing his face to crease with mirth as if to credit the speaker with an uncommon degree of wit. "She`ll be with you straight."

"He says to bring him a bottle of brandy," said Susan, coming from the private room, "so as not to have to trouble us again, being as busy as we are."

"Very thoughtful, I`m sure."

"He gave me this," she said, handing her father-in-law a coin, "and he said I needn`t bother taking him any change."

"A gentleman indeed," said the landlord, spinning the gold coin nimbly before catching it in his big hand and conveying it to the pocket of his apron. "Take him a bottle of the best, and then go and help Meg."

Presently, all the glasses and tankards recharged, and the newcomers settled and supplied, and their money collected, the landlord nodded to Sam to let him know that he might set off again.

"This is a longer ditty," said Sam, "and so that I don`t dry out in the middle of it, I`ll take enough to keep me warbling." He lifted his glass, and then just as it touched his lips, he stopped, and eyeing the expectant room, added, "and you may do the same."

"Good man!" thought the landlord. "Let them get it down their necks!"

"This one," said Sam, at last, "is about a poor young lad, who, as you will see, has lost his winder."

There was a ripple of salacious mirth at this. Anyone who came from Middleton knew that a winder was a winder of bobbins, but it didn`t prevent the collective wit of the gathering from sharing the expectation that a double meaning or two was to follow.

Where Gerrard's stream, with pearly gleam,

Runs down in gay meander,
A weaver boy, bereft of joy,
Upon a time did wander.

'Ah! well a day,' the youth did say,
'I wish I did not mind her,
I'm sure had she regarded me,
I ne'er had lost my winder.

The landlord watched the performance, confident that he knew how it would go. During the first verse, there had been enough of a twinkle in Sam's eye to suggest to those who were expecting a bit of bawdy that they weren't to be disappointed. But that was not how it would continue.

Her ready hand was white as milk,
Her fingers finely moulded,
And when she touch'd a thread of silk,
Like magic it was folded.

She turn'd her wheel, she sang her song,
And sometimes I have join'd her,
Oh that one strain would wake again
From thee my lovely winder.

And when the worsted hank she wound,
Her skill was further proved,
No thread uneven there was found,
Her bobbins never roved.

With sweet content, to work she went,
And looked not behind her,
With fretful eye for ills to spy;
But now I've lost my winder.

167

And never would she let me wait
When downing on a Friday,
Her wheel went at a merry rate,
Her person always tidy.

But she is gone, and I'm alone,
I know not where to find her,
I've sought the hill, the wood and rill,
No tidings of my winder.

I've sought her at the dawn of day,
I've sought her at the noonin',
I've sought her when the evening grey
Had brought the hollow moon in.

I've call'd her on the darkest night
With wizard spells to bind her,
And when the stars arose in light,
I've wander'd forth to find her.

Her hair was like the raven's plume
And hung in tresses bonny,
Her checks so fair did roses bear
That blush'd as sweet as ony.

With slender waist and carriage chaste,
Her looks were daily kinder,
I mourn and rave, and cannot weave
Since I have lost my winder.

There was a moment of rapt silence in the room, and then a clatter of generous applause. There was not one amongst this gathering of rough and tumble lads of Middleton who hadn`t been drawn into the lyrical sadness. Even the young gentleman traveller had stepped forward, briefly, to the doorway of the private room, to add to the applause.

"Shall I tell him to give it another five minutes?" said Meg, who pretty well knew the form.

"That`s right, and tell him to give them something a bit more bawdy next. They like something lyrical and sentimental, but they don`t like too much of it. They`re ready for a bit of bawdy next, but make sure their glasses are filled, and don`t forget to collect, because there are some who`ll let you."

"All right, father," she said, rolling her eyes. "I have done this before, you know."

"Yes, I know, I know," he conceded, patting her bottom gently.

"Don`t do that, father, I`ve bruises there enough tonight!"

At this point, the front door opened again, and in came another cohort, this time of drinkers who were more regularly customers at the Church Tavern.

"All right, lads," he said, wary that the Church Tavern drinkers had a reputation for being more rowdy, "you`re all very welcome, but we`re that full, you may have to stand. Meg, see what these lads want to drink."

Coming in, they sidled into places along the corridor, the smallest slipping through to the front, the tallest happy to stay at the back.

It was a good ten minutes before everyone was served, and then, as word went round to `hush`, Sam stood forward and prepared to begin a new recitation.

"I see we`ve a few lads down from the Church Tavern, tonight, then."

This was greeted with a chorus of good-natured jeers and whistles.

"What`s up lads, is the ale off? And from the Assheton, too. Well, what an honour this is! I`ve never known an Assheton drinker walk further than he has to get his ale. And uphill, too. Beer must have gone sour there, too. I say, Will, yours must be the only decent barrel in Middleton tonight. Right, now, I`ll beg a little quiet while I tell you a tale of a young lad from hereabouts who shall remain nameless…"

"That`ll be you, then, Sam!" heckled one in the crowd.

"Nay, Tom, I said I wouldn`t name you, but now I have to! So this young weaver goes on the runabout after falsely persuading a young maiden of the parish to part with her virtue, and this is his tale…"

He began, and after the first verse, the landlord smiled to himself. A nice bawdy ballad with plenty of innuendo and double meaning – just the job! It was at this point, that he noticed, standing at the back of the crowd in the corridor, Simon, the young lad who he knew had been taken in to work with the Bamfords.

"What do you want young`un?" he asked, sternly. He knew no harm of him, but there was something about the lad that he didn`t quite trust.

"I wanted a word with Sam," the lad replied.

"You can see he`s busy. You`ll not get near him for a bit yet. What is it? Do you want me to give him a message when he`s done?"

"No," said the lad.

"Well, I`m not having you lurking about here like a bad smell. If it won`t wait till he gets back home, you can wait for him by the door there, or outside. Go on, be sharp!"

The lad cocked his head as if in defiance, but when the landlord feinted to grab him by the collar, he backed off out of sight.

"Cheeky beggar," he muttered to himself.

`Twas nearly twelve months after, Sam was now continuing.
When the hue and cry died down
This gallant weaver lad thought fit
To come back home to town…

I`ve brought a present for you, Moll
Some ribbons bright and gay
So come and kiss me once again
For now I`m home to stay

A gift, she said, makes all things well,
And I`ve got one for thee
She brought three month baby in
To sit upon his knee...!

"He`ll be finished in a minute," said the landlord to his daughter-in-law, Susan. "Go in and see that the young gentleman`s all right, because it`s going to be like Bedlam in here shortly."

Sam brought his bawdy tale to a suitably moral conclusion, and gained his well-deserved applause.

"Take this to him, Meg," said the landlord, handing her a freshly filled tankard. "He`ll be wanting this."

"Is he right, Susan?"

"He`s gone. Must have gone to bed."

"Right. Never mind. Let`s start serving the hordes. Heaven help us, we`ll not be finished this side of midnight!"

171

Chapter 39

"**Y**ou must have been merry when you came in last night!" said Mima.

"I think I must have been," said Sam.

"To sleep down here with your boots on!"

"Well, you know what I`m like!" he said. "If I`d tried to get up them stairs, I would have woken the whole household up."

"I might have known you`d be thinking of others..."

"You`re not off me are you pet?"

"Course I`m not!" she said, pecking him on the forehead. "A man should have a good night out once in a while."

"Are you feeling better, chuck?"

"That I am. Slept like a babe. Now, you get up and take your boots off and put your head on a proper pillow for half an hour."

"No, I`m all right. I`ll just swill my face, and I`ll be right as rain."

Mima began to set the breakfast things out, and Sam, refreshed, after dousing his head from the rainwater butt in the yard, began to tell her the tale of the night. "They were in from the Assheton and the Church. I thought to myself, we should be selling tickets for this, make a small fortune!"

"Don`t let it go to your head!"

"No chance of that. When all`s said and done, a simple, honest frugal life`s what`s best."

He put his hand over hers warmly.

"Let`s make a pot of tea," she said. "I just fancy that, don`t you?"

"I do," said Sam.

It was only at eight o`clock, when the looms had been running for an hour, that it was discovered that Lucy was missing, and that from the state of it, it seemed her bed had not been slept in.

"Did she say anything to you, Simon?"

Simon, sitting sullenly at his winding, as if in a world of his own, shook his head.

"Maybe she rose early and made her bed and went out for a walk. I mean, she has been showing signs of wanting to get out and about, and really, you know, it`s no bad thing. She can`t be sitting around here all day, being waited on like a princess in a fairy tale."

"Don`t be harsh, Sam."

"I`m not being harsh. It`s true."

"Well, I`m sure you`re right. She`s just such a worry, that`s all."

"You`re too gentle, Mima. But don`t ever stop being so, It`s what I love you most for."

By ten o`clock, a rumour had started to circulate around Middleton that the body of a young woman, suspected to be a victim of murder, had been discovered in a clearing of the lower slopes of the Warren, just by the path, by a lad who, taking a short-cut, was running over that way to get to the schoolhouse on the other side of the brow. Going to the nearest place to report this, which was a bootmaker`s shop on the road below, he had been sent home, trembling, to his mother, and the bootmaker and his son had gone to find and then watch over the body until the constable could be fetched.

As it spread around the town the tale took on various additions and began to exist in several different versions. The woman had been found hanged, one version said, at the end of her own scarf; she had been found with her knees aloft and her skirts awry, in the attitude of one about to give birth, said another; aye, or about something else, added a cynical commentator to this. The only constant factor in the story was that the murdered female was wearing a crimson velveteen jacket and skirt, and that, lying near the body, was a hat with feathers.

By the time it reached the Bamford household, at about noon, and breaking in, as it did, on the growing concern that Lucy had not yet returned, its impact was devastating. That Lucy`s old clothes were gone was immediately ascertained. Mima screamed, and then, beside herself, sobbed uncontrollably. Simon, his face white, went outside, and was heard retching. Sam, putting his hands firmly around Mima`s shoulders, told her to be calm and to be strong.

"Go and see, Sam," she said.

Simon`s retching could still be heard outside.

"Go and see, Sam," she begged. "See if it`s her. See if it`s poor Lucy. I know it is, I know it in my heart, but go and see..."

Chapter 40

By the time Sam Bamford arrived at the scene, the constable and his deputy were trying to persuade a small crowd who`d gathered, curious to find out what they could and to catch a glimpse of the body, to keep their distance.

"It`s not a pretty sight. There`s nothing to be done. So best if you just go back home, and leave it to us. Eh, Tom? Eh, Martha?"

But they weren`t so easily persuaded, and if anything, the warning that it wasn`t a pretty sight served more to inflame than to dampen curiosity. There was much speculation about what sort of female might be out, late at night, wearing a crimson velveteen skirt and jacket, and a hat with a feather, and it was generally agreed that it must be the sort of female who was no better than she ought to be. When someone said that the girl Mima Bamford had rescued from the shambles and had taken into her home, was wearing such an outfit or something very similar, the flow of speculation started to run quickly into a whole new network of lurid channels.

When Sam Bamford himself was seen approaching from the stile, a guilty hush fell over the crowd.

"Come on, then, Sam," said the constable. "You`d best have a look and see what you can tell us."

The body was lying on its side, with one knee drawn over, but the upper part of the torso and the head were face upwards, with the arms thrown outwards. The hat had rolled off and lay two or three feet away.

"Is this how she was found?" asked Sam.

"We`ve not touched her, apart from pulling her skirts down a bit, for shame`s sake. People are saying it might be the girl you took in. Is it her?"

"Aye," said Sam, looking down at the green eyes, still open, as they must have been to look her last on the world, but now devoid of their lustre.

He kneeled beside the body. From close to, it was clear to see that the grass where her head lay was matted with quantities of dried blood.

"Poor Lucy," he said quietly. "You didn't deserve this."

Eventually the constable helped him up. "No good to be done now, eh, Sam?" he said, in a kindly way. "You'd best get back and comfort Mima. I expect she'll need it."

"What's to be done with her?" he asked.

Well, the truth was that the constable, at this moment in time, was as much in the dark as anyone else about what was to be done with her, but he rather suspected that it was going to turn out to be a bother and an inconvenience. A body turning up in mysterious circumstances, probably murdered, wasn't something that happened very often, and it was something that those in authority were very reluctant to take responsibility for, in case it rendered them, or the parish, liable for expenses. He'd even heard of one case where a Justice had ordered the constable to have the body secretly carried away to be deposited in a neighbouring parish, for them to deal with.

"What do you think, then, Mattie?" he said to his fellow, after Sam Bamford had agreed to go home, and whilst they awaited the arrival of Joseph Lime, the coroner, or one of the magistrates, or Lord Suffield, all of whom had been notified.

"How do you mean, John?"

The constable nodded towards the body. After Sam's departure, and now having a good enough tale to tell, most of the crowd had dissipated, too, leaving the two of them, as they kept up their vigil, with time on their hands in which to speculate. "What would you say happened?"

Mattie looked about, weighing up the scene. "Difficult to say."

"Struck from behind by person or persons unknown," said John, airing his knowledge of legal jargon.

"That about sums it up, I reckon."

"The thing is, with a murder, and let's face it, we don't see that many of them hereabouts, you generally know straight away who it is: a crazed husband, a jealous wife, a neighbour with a grudge, but in this case, we know next to nothing."

"Well, it's not our business to find out. Leave that to our betters, eh?"

"What's this!" said John, suddenly. During his explanation of the complexities as he saw them, he had been helping his thought processes by walking around. What he now saw, half-hidden in the fallen leaves, was the cause of his exclamation.

"What's what?" said Mattie.

John kneeled forward, picked up an object, and then held it aloft. It was a piece of wood, a natural piece of wood of the kind you might see fallen from a tree, but the size and weight of a club, and at one end the bark was covered in blood.

"Here," said John, with minor triumph, "unless I'm mistaken, is the murder weapon."

He brought it close for Mattie's inspection. "Now what does this tell us?"

Mattie thought carefully about this before venturing his opinion, and John waited, expectantly but patiently.

"Well," said Mattie, at last, "that she was hit on the back of the head with it."

"Precisely," said John.

Mattie thought again. "But didn't we know that already?"

"No," said John. "We only surmised. For all we know, in ipsum factus, she might have been running fast, tripped, fallen headlong and smashed her head against a gnarled root. But what we do know for sure now, is that she was murdered, and what else do we know?"

"You'd better tell me, John, because I haven't got the wit for this sort of thing."

"What we know now is that the murder wasn`t committed with malice aforethought."

"What does that mean?"

"It wasn`t planned."

"How do we know that?"

"Because of the weapon. This blood-stained log wasn`t brought to the scene, was it? It was picked up from where nature had left it, on the spur of the moment. It`s what`s called, in legal parlance, an adventitious weapon. So, the question is, was she pursued and struck as she ran away from someone, or was she caught in fragrantis delectum?"

"What`s fragrantis delectum?"

"If it was you or me it would be with your trousers down, in her case it`s as might be surmised from how we found her skirts before we tidied her up a bit."

"Oh, I see."

John nodded his head, slowly, wisely. "In which case, we`re talking about a third party, a jealous lover, maybe, someone for whom the sight of her in delectum might have inspired a sudden rage. He picks up the log, and before he knows what he`s done he`s knocked her brains out."

"But what I don`t understand," said Mattie, much impressed by John`s reasoning powers and trying hard to keep up, "is this. If she was caught in delectus…"

"Delectum," John corrected.

"In delectum. Well, wouldn`t her head have been down on the ground as on a pillow, and so how could the back of her head have been dashed in by an adventitious weapon?"

John looked at Mattie for some time, shaking his head sadly. "How long have you been wed, Mattie?"

"Eighteen months."

He shook his head again. "You need to buck up your ideas then," he said. "You`ve a lot to learn yet."

"But the other thing is this," said Mattie, now quite warmed to the pursuit of truth. "Could it not be that the murder was planned, and that the murderer, knowing the lie of the land where his crime was to be committed, said to himself, in his malice aforethought, I don`t need to take a weapon because I know there`ll be no shortage of adventitious ones to hand as soon as I want one?"

"You`ve got no idea, have you," said John, flatly, and a little sadly. "No idea at all."

It was at this point that Joseph Stone, the local coroner, who drew a regular stipend but was very seldom called on to act, and Thomas Livesey, the only one of the town`s three magistrates who could be found, appeared on the scene.

They were followed by Arthur Lumb, the town`s undertaker, and Will Robin, the landlord of the Boar`s Head, who, having heard a lot of rumours and nonsense, wanted to know what was going on.

"You should listen to John," said Mattie. "He`s got it sized up, pretty well, haven`t you, John?"

Taking his cue, John stepped forward. "Now this, as I discovered," said the Constable, brandishing the blood-stained club, "unless I`m mistaken, which I think I`m not, is the murder weapon."

"Yes, well, never mind that," said the coroner, so troubled with gout and bile that it was only dedication to duty that had brought him out at all. "We can see how she died. The question is, what`s to be done with the body?"

"Can you take her?" said Thomas Livesey to the undertaker.

"I can take her this minute. You only have to say the word. But the question is this, because the moment I take her I begin to incur costs, and the longer I keep her the greater those costs are liable to be, so the question is: if I take her, who is going the defray those costs?"

"If, as I`ve heard it said," suggested the magistrate, "she was of the household of Samuel Bamford, might not he be prepared to defray the costs?"

"Well, so he might," said the undertaker, "but until I have word and assurances of that, it would not be my position to anticipate or to intervene."

"Can she be brought to a room at the Boar`s Head, Mr Robin, pending such assurances?"

Will Robin shook his head. "Put yourself in the position of my customers," he said. "It may sound harsh, but they`ll not want to sup where there`s been a corpse laid out."

"Well, the body can`t stay here, can it," said the magistrate, in exasperation. "what`s to become of it?"

"Don`t worry about the body," said Oliver Canky, the sexton, emerging from the shadows of the path. "Let me take care of that."

Chapter 41

"I warned your father," said Lady Mary. "I told him it would come to this!"

William Harbord, the second Lord Suffield, closed his eyes, and, leaning his head slightly forward, squeezed the top of his nose between finger and thumb.

"Once you start setting up market-places you invite all sorts of rabblement and raggle-taggle gypsies, and they're like vermin, easy to attract and impossible to get rid of."

"The country depends on markets, mother, it's where people sell what they have made or produced, and buy what they need. That's how the country runs!"

"In towns and cities, yes, but Middleton is a village, or at least was a village, hardly that, and so it should have remained."

"You're living in the past, mother. But anyway, I fail to see what any of this has to do with today's events, unfortunate as those events may be."

They were sitting in the dining-room at Middleton Hall, and just at the point where, having made polite conversation through dinner, and for half an hour afterwards, he thought he might make his excuses and spend the hour he had promised himself in the billiard room, she had brought this up again. It seemed that whenever some ripple of disquiet, however minor, passed over the surface of her mind, she traced it back to his father's efforts to bring some modernisation to the sleepy backwater that Middleton had been in the 1770s and 80s – still was, to a large extent. It was a fixed idea that nothing would shift, and though one should allow the elderly their whims and eccentricities, it was, nevertheless, at times, annoying.

"Whores and murderers roaming free!" she muttered with a renewed access of moral outrage.

He regretted now telling her anything about it. When the message had come from the constable, that morning, he had been of the opinion that it was something with which the local Justices should be quite capable of dealing without needing any assistance from him. That was his opinion still, and he had only mentioned it to his mother because he knew she would hear about it, from Mrs Canky or some other such gossiping tongue, sooner or later.

"It wouldn`t have happened in your grandfather`s time!"

William closed his eyes again, a little wearily, convinced now that he should have left it to Mrs Canky, thereby gaining at least a period of grace for himself, however short.

"You make it sound, mother, as if grandfather was some sort of King Arthur presiding over a noble and harmonious Camelot where all was just and good. Was Middleton ever such an Arcadian idyll?"

"I didn`t say it was an Arcadian idyll. What I`m saying is that your grandfather knew who all the people were, he took an interest in them, and they took their morality from him as much as they took it from the church."

"Mother! A young woman, by all accounts a common prostitute, who, had not the Bamfords taken her in, would also probably have been a vagrant, has been found dead, probably murdered, but by whom we have no idea, and probably never will have. It is regrettable, but it has happened, as such things do, from time to time. It is not, essentially, a Middleton matter."

"Of course it`s a Middleton matter!" replied his mother in an almost venomous retort. "It happened in Middleton, didn`t it? How can it not be a Middleton matter?"

"But I don`t understand, mother, what it is that you want me to do."

"What I want you to do, William, is to take some responsibility. You are, whether you like it or not, the Lord of the Manor, and for you to take responsibility will show people that such things do not go unnoticed. It will reassure people that there is a care, and that care is being exercised."

"But what is it, exactly, mother, that you want me to do?"

"Oh, come, William! You`re a man, and I`m a weak old woman. Do you expect me to explain everything to you!"

"I`m going to the billiard room," said William, getting up, suddenly and decisively, and leaving the room.

Lady Mary smiled faintly, and then called Tessa, her maid.

"Very nasty business, isn`t it, milady?" said Tessa.

"It is indeed, Tessa," said Lady Mary. "But I`m sure that Lord Suffield will see to it that the right things are done."

"That`s very reassuring to hear, your ladyship, very reassuring, indeed."

"Yes," said Lady Mary, with quiet and very dignified satisfaction, though she could not help but think, in the region of private thought where curiosity vied with rank and responsibility, that it would be very interesting to find out, when she next saw her, what Mrs Canky thought of all this.

Chapter 42

By mid-morning, the next day, word was spreading that Lord Suffield, together with Justice Livesey and two other magistrates of the town, was to set up a bench, and that Will Robin had agreed that the Sessions room at the Old Boar`s Head, quite correctly, could be made ready for that purpose.

The Justices, having never had to deal with a case like this before, were in some confusion about how to proceed. Petty disputes between neighbours, where one brought a case against another over, say, the ownership of a strip of land, or alleged damage caused by a stray animal, or drunken and disorderly behaviour causing a breach of the peace – these were matters in which they were confident of knowing what due process entailed - and, in fact, to make life rather easier, in nine cases out of ten the warring parties were persuaded, when the original anger or indignation had cooled, that a settlement out of court was by far the least troublesome way of finding a resolution.

"We have a victim," said Justice Livesey, "but we have no-one bringing a prosecution, and we have no defendant. I`m at a loss to know how we begin."

"Unless Bamford wishes to bring a prosecution...?" said Justice Tanner. "As having, as it were, if I`ve heard correctly, put himself in a position of guardianship over the wretched creature."

"Let that be as it may," replied Justice Livesey. "But we still have no defendant."

Justice Gilbert, sitting between them, and showing signs that his hardness of hearing had not improved since the last bench was called, simply nodded, as if agreeing with each position taken by his colleagues.

"If I may make a suggestion…" said Lord Suffield, sitting at the table beside them. The three Justices turned respectfully towards him. "What is important, gentlemen, is that as many of the facts relevant to the case are assembled, by yourselves, here today, so that no-one should be in any doubt that a heinous crime such as this, notwithstanding the corrupt and degenerate nature of the victim, will be properly investigated."

"That`s all very well, your lordship," said Justice Livesey, taking care, as he made his reservation, to lose none of the deference due to Lord Suffield. "But how are we to assemble facts without a prosecutor to put them and a defendant to challenge them?"

"Let it be done in this way," said Lord Suffield. "Send word about the town that any man, or woman, for that matter, who has any knowledge pertaining to this business, should come forward, and make it known to yourselves and to his fellow townsfolk. When that is done, we will then see how to proceed next."

Justice Gilbert nodded wholehearted agreement to this; the other two Justices had serious reservations, but did not express them, and so it was agreed that this was the way to set about things, and a message was immediately sent to Sam Bamford`s house, asking him to be so good as to attend the meeting of the Justices at the Boar`s Head.

Whilst they were awaiting his arrival, the landlord of the inn, Will Robin came forward, and informed the bench of a circumstance which he had just remembered, which the honourable gentleman might think it worth their while to hear. The deceased, he said, had made an appearance at the inn some days since, he couldn`t remember how many but it couldn`t be much above a week, if that, and that he now remembered her because of the clothes he`d seen on the body the previous day.

"But the thing is this," he added. "The next day – I'm pretty sure it was the next day, though I couldn't swear to it, a rough looking fellow came here asking for her."

"And did you recognise this man?"

"No, sir. I think I know most men from Middleton, and roundabout Middleton, in fact I dare say I know all of them, I'd go as far as that, but I've never seen that man before."

"And you say he was a rough looking man?"

"Big fellow, brawny. Yes, I'd say rough. I think that's as good a word for him as any."

"Thank you, Mr Robin. If you remember anything else, you will let us know."

"Yes, your worships. May I ask your worships if any refreshments will be required by your worships because if so, I'll set about it straight away."

It was unanimously agreed by the three men of the bench that some refreshments would be appropriate, in about an hour's time.

A period of quietness now fell on the room, as they waited for the arrival of Sam Bamford, and those of the public who had chosen to stay and be witnesses of the proceedings began to talk amongst themselves. There was then a murmur that Joe Robinson, owd Scrat as he was known to most people of the town, had come into the Boar's Head, accompanied by Oliver Canky, the sexton, and that Scrat, having heard of the proceedings, had come to give information to the bench.

"Joseph Howarth," he said, when asked, for formal purposes, what his name was.

"And why do you come here, Mr Howarth?" asked Justice Livesey.

"I live up yonder, on the Warren, as people know," said Scrat. "And I knew nothing of this matter until yesterday afternoon when I returned from some business with Mr Canky which had kept me overnight in Manchester, and was informed of it by Mr Canky's wife."

"Then if you were in Manchester, Mr Howarth, how can you help us?"

"Only in this respect," said Scrat. "Some nights since, on my way home, I was accosted, just across the way from here by a woman who, according to the account given to me by Mrs Canky, may well have been, in respect of the clothing she was wearing, the woman who was found in unfortunate circumstances yesterday."

"In what way did she accost you, Mr Howarth?"

"In a way that would shame me to mention, as I see that Mr and Mrs Bamford have just come into the room, but in a way, let it suffice to say, that I had to repulse in the sternest of terms."

"And you`ve not seen her since?"

"I have not."

"Thank you, Mr Howarth."

Scrat demonstrated, by every facial expression known to the humble man, that no thanks were necessary, and was then assisted from the room by his friend, Mr Canky.

"I found her in the market place," said Mima Bamforth, "and in so pitiful a condition that I could not have left her there, no Christian soul could, but I took her back."

"Into your own home."

"Into my husband`s home, but yes, knowing that I would have his blessing to bring her there."

The eyes in the room turned, momentarily, towards Sam Bamford. What those eyes did not fully realise was that in looking at Sam Bamford they were looking at a man who was feeling some relief. He had come, as requested, to the hearing, thinking that he might need, to be clear in his own conscience, to inform it of his first meeting with Lucy when Joe Howarth`s name had been mentioned. Now that Scrat had come forward himself, he felt absolved of that responsibility.

"And what did you do for her, Mrs Bamford, during the short time she was kept under your roof?"

"Put her into fresh clothes, gave her food, tried to bring her to see the error of her ways."

"And did your efforts meet with any success?"

"It was such a short time, but yes, so I thought. She seemed mindful of what goodness was intended to her, and she was learning one or two things of usefulness. We hoped, Sam and me, that she might eventually find work as a spinner or a winder, and replant herself in proper soil. She was a good girl once, and of a good family, and her misfortunes..."

Here, Mima Bamford, overcome with emotion, was unable to carry on.

"What my wife means," said Sam, putting his arm round her shoulder to comfort her, "is that her misfortunes weren`t all of her own making. She was driven from her place of birth by want, like many more, in these times, and chance brought her where the only people who offered to help her were the same who helped to bring her into degradation."

"Quite so," said Lord Suffield. "And yet it seems, judging from the fact that she was wearing the garb of her former occupation, that she intended to return to it."

"It may seem so, your lordship," said Sam, "but yet, it is not certain. And I can`t believe that she went out at night because she intended to be murdered."

There was a ripple of mirth in the room at this, quickly stifled by a sharp look from Lord Suffield.

"Did she give you any warning that she intended to go out alone on the night in question?"

"No."

"Was anything missing from the house?" asked Justice Livesey.

"Missing?"

"Any money, any rings or jewellery – anything that might have had a ready value?"

"We`re not wealthy people, sir. There`s nothing of value in the house besides our looms and some books, but no, if anything was missing we would have noticed."

Justice Livesey looked to the others on the bench, and to Lord Suffield to see if there were any other questions they wished to ask, but they shook their heads – apart from Justice Gilbert, who nodded his, though it was taken to mean the same thing.

"Thank you, Mr Bamford, and Mrs Bamford."

At this point, there being no further witnesses, the townsfolk who had stayed to observe repaired to the tap room, and the refreshments promised by Mr Robin, the landlord, were brought through for the dignitaries of the bench.

"I think we may find," said Justice Tanner, "that our business is all but done."

"I`m of the same opinion," said Justice Livesey. "I can`t see that anyone else will come forward now who hasn`t done so already."

"May we set a time limit, do you think, Lord Suffield?"

Lord Suffield was minded to agree. He had done what he could to assert what his mother had termed `some authority` but he was under no real illusion that it was going to get them anywhere.

"After all," said Justice Tanner, "the girl was little more than an unreclaimed street walker, and though it seems harsh to say it, whoever did this, the world can hardly be said to be a worse place for it."

"I`d put a wager on it being the rough fellow, the one the landlord spoke of."

"Well, I agree. But there we are. No name. No whereabouts. No known acquaintance. We may sit here all day but I don`t think any amount of sitting here will get us any closer to discovering him."

"We`ll give it until two o`clock," said Lord Suffield, who, though he felt obliged to meet some of what was said with a frown, did not necessarily disagree with any of it.

As two o`clock approached, the atmosphere in the sessions room had become one of apathy and indolence. There were some of the townsfolk, who, talking amongst themselves and agreeing that the best of it was probably done, had not returned after the break. The Justices, who had run out of things to say to each other, were lost in their own thoughts. Justice Livesey was trying to recall an old tune that had somehow got lost in his head; Justice Tanner was drumming his fingers on the table as if to recreate a military tattoo; Justice Gilbert, as ever, was nodding his head, as if he had left it on permanent nodding duty to make sure that he was not deemed to have missed anything. Lord Suffield was picturing, in all its splendid detail, the cricket gallery at Middleton Hall, and recalling a couple of very fine knocks he`d made there, with his brother bowling, when they were on holiday there as boys.

He had just taken out his fob watch, and was thinking of a few words with which to bring proceedings to a formal conclusion, when the door opened, and Ezekiel Barton, with his son, James, was ushered past the constables and into the room by the ever-obliging landlord.

Those on the bench sat up, straightening themselves, as it were, into a dignified bearing which had been allowed to slip, but which was now required again.

"Do you have something for us, Mr Barton?" asked Justice Livesey. "Some information?"

"My son has," said Ezekiel Barton, who immediately sat down and dabbed his forehead, perspiring, it seemed, with the effort of hastening to the hearing.

The young man, conscious that the eyes in the room were now focused on him, shrugged his shoulders. "It`s probably nothing," he said.

"Well, tell us what it is, and let us be the judge of that."

"I saw them," said James Barton. "I didn`t think anything of it, but when I heard that a woman had been murdered and heard a description, I thought it must be the woman I`d seen. I mentioned it to my father and he said I should come here."

"You referred just now, though, if I heard you correctly, to more than one person."

"Yes, the woman and a boy."

"You`d better tell us the circumstances."

"Well, it was about nine o`clock, the night before last. I can`t remember exactly what the time was, but it can`t have been any later, as it was still light enough to see. Anyway, I`d been to the Church Tavern, for a little refreshment and company, you understand, and I was making my way down towards here, to the Old Boar`s Head, I mean, where I`d heard there was a bit of a show going on."

"Yes?"

"Well, that`s when I saw them. The young woman and the lad, and I noticed them in particular because they were in the middle of a flaming row about something. Cussing and accusing each other with all manner of lewd stuff and what not! I passed them by, and said something about minding the peace, and then went on my way and left them to go on theirs."

"And you came here, to the Boar`s Head."

"Well, no, I didn`t as a matter of fact. I intended to, but I`d had a few drinks already, and seeing this unseemly behaviour, I was minded to think of the evils of drunkenness, and so I changed my mind and walked straight home."

"Very correct," said Justice Livesey. "Very commendable. And the young man, or the boy, as you describe him, was, presumably, someone not known to you."

"No, sir..."

"...Not known to you?"

"No, sir. What I mean is that no, he wasn`t somebody unknown to me."

191

"Try to make yourself clear, Mr Barton."

"Well, he called her Lucy, and she called him Simon. It was the boy who does Sam Bamford`s errands. Simon."

The members of the bench exchanged looks, and those in the room who had been on the point of leaving, thinking that they`d go home with nothing to report other than that it had been a pretty disappointing day, now sat up, galvanised by this new revelation.

Justice Livesey nodded to the constable. "Go again to Sam Bamford`s house, and tell him that his lad, Simon`s presence is required at this hearing without any delay."

Chapter 43

The news that Simon, Sam Bamford`s strange lad had been called to the hearing to give an account of himself, together with the expectation that new revelations of a lurid nature were about to be divulged, spread quickly through the town. By the time he came through the door, with Sam Bamford at his side, the two constables and the landlord were already busy establishing order amongst the noisy crowd who had now gathered, and were eagerly awaiting the drama they supposed was about to happen. It was some minutes, as people still crowded in, before Justice Livesey was able to make himself heard calling for order, and it took three sharp knocks on the table from Lord Suffield`s cane to still the racket.

All the time, Simon stood there, white-faced, looking first towards the bench and then towards Sam for some reassurance.

"Now," said Justice Livesey, at last, "don`t be put off by there being so many people here, all that`s required of you is to tell us what`s true, and if you do that, you need have nothing to fear. Do you understand that?"

"Yes," came the reply, in a very faint voice.

"How old are you Simon?"

"Fifteen."

"Fifteen. That`s old enough to know the difference between truth and lying. You do understand that difference don`t you Simon?"

"Yes."

"Good. Now, you were seen, the night before last, not far from here, with a young woman."

"With Lucy, yes."

"Indeed, with Lucy. And is it true that you were having an altercation with Lucy, an argument, or cross words?"

"Yes."

"What about?"

Simon looked again towards Sam and Mima, who both nodded, encouraging him to continue.

"She`d put on her old clothes. She was going to go out without telling Sam and Mima. I was trying to tell her not to go."

"This was when you were still at the house?"

"Yes."

"But she didn`t heed your advice?"

"No, she was set on going."

"So then you followed her from the house."

"Yes. She was going off. She wasn`t going to come back. I thought she was going back to her old ways, and she was angry with me for following her, and that`s when we had the row."

"And that`s what it was about?"

"Yes."

"It wasn`t a lovers` tiff then?"

"No," said Simon, colouring slightly.

The Justice looked at him steadily, nodding his head slowly, as if, by some process of his own thinking, he was minded to conclude that the answer, despite the lad`s embarrassment, an honest one.

Lord Suffield now interposed, and in a rather more peremptory tone than the Justice. "Did you say anything to Mr or Mrs Bamford that night when you got back?"

"No."

"And did you say anything the next morning, or the next afternoon, after you knew that Lucy had been killed?"

"No."

"That seems very strange. You say you were concerned for Lucy, and tried to prevent her coming into harm`s way, and yet at no point did you say anything of what you knew?"

"No."

"Why?"

"I was frightened."

"Frightened of what?"

"Of getting into trouble."

"Into trouble for what, if you`d done nothing wrong?"

Simon looked again towards Sam and Mima, his eyes filling with alarm.

"Well? What had you done that you were so afraid to speak of?"

"Nothing," said Simon, his voice cracking and letting out something between a cry and a squeak.

"The boy`s confused," said Ezekiel Barton, rising from his chair, and intervening on his behalf. "Give him time to think."

"Very well. You may have a few moments to compose your thoughts. Bring him a glass of water, Mr Robin."

The landlord picked his way through to the door and to the public bar, deserted apart from his daughter who was talking in a way which appeared somewhat flirtatious, with the young gentleman who, if he stayed another night, would now owe him three days` lodging and stabling.

"Come on now, Meg," he said. "You`d better run along the road and bring Susan. It`s going to be mayhem in here when they`re done."

"Why, what`s going on?"

"I haven`t time to tell you, now. I`ve to take a glass of water back directly for the witness, or the accused, more like, I could say!"

Again, it required three sharp raps of Lord Suffield`s cane to bring the hubbub to a level where the voices from the bench could be heard. Simon, who had been allowed to sit down to have a sip from his glass of water, was now instructed to stand again.

"Now, then, Simon," said Justice Livesey, "you`ve had a little time to think, and now I must ask you again what it was that you were so frightened of that you didn`t say anything to Mr Bamford about what you knew of Lucy`s flight."

"But I did," said Simon, suddenly. "I did try to tell him."

"How did you try to tell him?"

"I came in here. I came into the tap-room, or tried to, but he was reciting a poem and it was so packed with folk I couldn`t get past to get anywhere near him."

"That`s true," said the landlord. "Now that he`s mentioned it, I remember. He did come in, asking for Sam. And I told him to wait by the door or in the back corridor, but when I looked again, he`d gone."

At this admission by the landlord, there was a stir in the room, a muttering almost of disappointment that with this technical detail the case against Simon had suddenly slipped away. A single rap of Lord Suffield`s cane was enough, this time, to bring about a silence.

"You came here with an important message for Mr Bamford," he said directly to Simon, "but you didn`t wait for him to finish his turn so that you could deliver this message?"

Simon looked steadily at Lord Suffield as if mesmerised by the directness of his stare, and then shook his head faintly.

"Where did you go?"

Simon remained silent.

"Where did you go, what did you do?"

"Did you go straight home?" suggested Justice Livesey, certain that such an effeminate looking creature couldn`t possibly have committed such an atrocious act.

"Did you go straight home?" echoed Lord Suffield.

A puzzled, troubled look came over Simon`s face.

"Did you go straight home?" said Lord Suffield, again, his voice now strident.

"I can`t remember," he said, in a barely audible voice.

"You can`t remember, that seems very strange."

"I can`t remember," Simon insisted, and then, suddenly, he turned and made a dash towards the door. For a moment there

196

was chaos, as he thrashed about against the attempts of the constables to seize him, but he was quickly subdued.

Lord Suffield, quickly realising that no amount of raps from his cane would bring things back to a decent semblance of order at this pass, instructed the constables that Simon was to be bound over, locked up and watched for the night, and after consulting the three Justices, announced that the hearing, now as a formal session of the magistrates, would reconvene the following morning.

Chapter 44

M rs Canky was in one of her shrewish fits, and Canky was on the receiving end.

"What was you doing in Manchester on business overnight with Scrat?" she demanded to know.

"I wasn`t in Manchester with Scrat."

"That`s where you said you was."

"It`s not where I said I was."

"How do I know I can believe you?"

"You know you can believe me, because I was here with you."

This stopped Mrs Canky for a moment, but the shrewish fits were such that their energy, like that of a wheel running freely downhill, wasn`t to be quickly ended, even by incontrovertible reason.

"If you were here with me, why did you tell them, at the trial – for this is what I`ve heard – that you were away on business with Scrat in Manchester."

"I didn`t tell them that. I didn`t tell them anything. Scrat told them that. And it`s not a trial, either, not a proper one, anyway."

"Just a minute," said Mrs Canky, "never mind whether it was a trial, a proper one or whatever other type of trial there is, how was it that Scrat said he was in Manchester with you when you was here with me, that`s what I want to know."

"Because he needed someone to vouch for him."

Mrs Canky furrowed her brow.

"Why would he need that?"

"Because a pox-ridden little whore was found with her pox-ridden little head bashed in not two hundred yards from where he lives. You know what a queer fish people think he is at the best of times. If you sling mud at him, it sticks. That's why."

Mrs Canky seemed again, momentarily at least, arrested in the progress of her shrewish fit, but Canky knew better than to suppose that it had yet blown itself out entirely.

"But you do go to Manchester with him, sometimes, don't you, and I don't see you until the next morning, so how do I know that you're not off consorting with the same type of pox-ridden whore that you talk of coming here in order to be murdered."

"You know what I am, don't you, Jenny?" appealed Oliver Canky, with all the honesty he could summon. "I'm a sexton. It's a humble job, but an honourable and a necessary job, and a decent one. I do what's needed for people, and they know that, and sometimes people make me a small gift. 'Here Canky,' they say, 'take this this little ring as a token of our esteem, take this bracelet, this bangle, but promise us solemnly you'll be on the watch-out to make sure his grave is not disturbed, make sure she lies still,' and that's what I do."

"I don't see why this takes you to Manchester."

"It takes me to Manchester because if I tried to sell those trinkets here, there'd be some people who'd say, 'now where did Canky get that from? Ten to a penny he slipped it off a finger that was already cold!' That's why I sometimes go to Manchester, and because I can get a better price there, too."

"How do I know I can believe you?"

"If I showed you something that I'm soon to take to Manchester, would you believe me?"

"What is it?"

Canky reached into his pocket, and, unwrapping his handkerchief, showed her a ring with a bright green stone and some glass beads of the same colour.

Jenny Canky let out an involuntary sigh as the light caught them.

"What do you think of those?" said Canky.

"Beautiful."

"Those are emeralds, Jen."

"Emeralds," she repeated, as if the very word was awe-inspiring.

"So now you can see why I have to go to Manchester."

"Emerald is my birth stone. Let me try them on, Oliver."

"If you tried them on you`d never want to part with them."

"I would. If I could once just try them, it would be enough."

"Go on then."

He watched as she slipped the ring onto her finger, and then he placed the beads around her neck.

"Do they suit me, Oliver?"

"They suit you so well, my little Jenny Wren, that I can hardly bear to take them off you."

"I`ll only wear them in the house, I promise."

"And so you must."

"You know what I think, Oliver. I think if I was to wear these at a certain time, when you`re being a proper husband to me, and me a proper wife, it might bring us luck."

"Very well, then," he said.

"I can hardly wait," she said, throwing her arms round his neck, and pressing herself amorously against him.

"Not just now, Jen," he said, patting her haunch. "I`ve business to see to tonight. There`s that murdered girl still lying in my store in the church vault, and I need to arrange for her to be watched over."

"All right, I`ll let you off, then. You`d better just hope the devil doesn't call before you get back!"

Turning out of his gate, Canky made his way along the ginnel that led upwards, crossing the lower corner of the Warren, towards the church yard and the church. It was a cold night, with a hint of frost in the air, with a clear sky and a bright moon, with starlight besides. Not a good night for the trade, but good in other respects. Taking out his keys, he unlocked the door to his store and struck a tinder to light the candle. As the flame grew steady, a suitably ghastly light glimmered on the walls, revealing the outline of the draped figure on the table. Stepping forward, he pulled the sheet back, and, their work now done, he lifted the two small pieces of lead from her eyes. The brow was ice-cold to his touch, as were the hands and the feet. `Good!` he muttered to himself. `You`ll do for a few days yet, my beauty.` He quickly checked the crimson velveteen jacket and skirt to make sure he hadn`t missed anything the day before. You never knew with whores – they seemed to have pockets everywhere to hide things away in. There was nothing. He tidied her up, pulled the white sheet over, and put weights round it to keep any vermin off her in the meantime, and then blew out the candle.

Locking the padlock, he walked on, down through the paddock towards the Boar`s Head. By tomorrow night, he reckoned, or the night after that, he would need to be organising a party for the river. That was part of his business tonight.

He was fairly sure that Ned Small would be in the Boar`s Head, and with any luck Sam Forcher and Bill Nimmy, would be, too. He`d already decided to exclude Scrat from this particular trip on the river. Ever since the night when they`d given Daniel Dyson the blacksmith`s lad his send-off, Scrat had been a bag of nerves, and he knew enough to suspect that it was all to do with the whore he`d been fretting about then, the same whore, if he wasn`t mistaken as the one he`d just tucked up in her winding-sheet. Whether or not Scrat actually had it in him to pick up a cudgel and bludgeon her off, he didn`t know, though he supposed most men were capable of most things if they were in it deep enough. Anyway, now that it looked as if the queer lad was going to drop for it, it didn`t matter anyway. But he didn`t want Scrat on duty tomorrow night, or any night soon, for that matter. He`d be the weak link in the chain. Hopefully, Sam and Ned and Billy would be up for it. He didn`t want to go himself, especially after the words he`d just had with Jenny, but if need be he`d have to.

As far as Will Robin, the landlord of the Boar`s Head was concerned, it was a question of making hay while the sun shines.

"How many more nights are you going to be wanting my Susan this week!" said his son, Ben, laughing.

"Don`t you complain!" said Will.

"I`m not complaining. As long as she`s in here serving, I don`t see why I can`t be in here supping. That`s what I tell her mother anyway."

"I`ll tell you what though, son, if trade keeps up like this, I shall have all the young widows in the parish after me for my fortune, aye, and a few maidens, too, I shouldn`t wonder!"

Many of those who`d been in the sessions room to witness the afternoon`s drama had stayed on; some had gone home and then come back again, bringing with them others who didn`t want to miss out on any meaty gossip, and by nine o`clock the pub was as full as it had been on the night when Sam Bamford had done his recitation.

"My money was on the brute who came looking for her, the one Will was on about."

"Aye, and he was a brute, too," said another.

"Why did you see him?"

"I saw him. As true as I`m standing here, and you`re standing there. Big brawny lad, looked like a navvy, with a foraging cap on."

"Aye. Come to think of it, when I cast my mind back, I think I caught a glimpse of him, too. Just there by the bar. Solid face with big flared nostrils."

So it went on, and before five minutes was out, there wasn`t anyone in the company at that table who hadn`t found, somewhere in his recollection, a glimpse of the fellow Will had described, and by the time all the details they supplied were put together you could have been forgiven for thinking it wasn`t just a brute of a man they were talking of but a mythical giant who`d come down a mythical beanstalk in search of Lucy.

"Anyroad," said one at last. "it`s all as one, because it`s not him as is under lock and key tonight, and it`s not him as will be standing before the bench tomorrow morning either…"

At another table, they were debating the unexpected arrival of David Barton, and the crucial testimony he`d given.

"What made him turn up, then, do you think?"

"I`ll tell you what made him turn up, his father made him turn up, and do you want me to tell you why?"

"Go on, then, I expect you will anyway."

"Well, look at it this way. Say he hadn`t turned up and then it came out later that he`d seen the girl that night. It might even have been young Simon who remembered seeing Barton`s lad there or thereabouts, and then the boot would have been on the other foot, wouldn`t it?"

"Are you saying it might have been him that did her in?"

"I`m saying, other things being equal, that that`s the way it might have looked. And Ezekiel Barton had the sense to see that, because I`m sure that lad of his hasn`t two grains of sense to rub together."

In the shadowy corner by the window, Oliver Canky was in a different conversation with Ned Small and Bill Nimmy.

"You think it`ll be tomorrow, then?"

"I think they`ll conclude on it tomorrow, but I`m setting it for the night after. That`ll give me time to get word to Strangeways for the delivery. Are you in?"

"I`m in," said Bill Nimmy.

"Ned?"

Ned Small screwed up his face. "I`m sorry, Canky, but I`m going to pass on this one. Too dangerous."

"How so?"

"You get caught with a body, that`s one thing, but get caught with a body who`s been murdered it begins to look like it`s all part of the same job."

Oliver Canky made a scornful snuff of laughter through his nose. "Do you think if I`d come upon little girl lost on the Warren and decided to do her in for the trade, I would have left her there for all this song and dance to be made about her? She`d have been stowed away and ready for the river before anybody even missed her. Anyway, who`s talking about getting caught?"

"I`m not saying that, Canky. I`m just saying how it might look."

"Very well, if you`ve decided suddenly to have dainty morals..."

"What about Scrat?" said Bill Nimmy.

Canky shook his head.

"That`s another thing," said Ned. "I mean it`s not a week since he was vexing himself over a fancy who`d turned up and now this. And I`ll tell you something else, he had a sweat on him in the court this morning."

"He`s in the clear," said Canky, dismissively. "He was with me."

"I`m not saying that. I`m just saying how it might look."

"You still in Bill?"

"I`m still in."

"Right, then. Will you go and see Sam Forcher for me?"

"I will."

"So," said Ned, "you think Bamford`s lad`ll swing for this, do you?"

The same question, at different times, was being put at other tables in the crowded, buzzing room.

"It looks bad for him, anyroad, doesn`t it?"

"Well, he wouldn`t answer the question, would he?"

"All he had to do was say he went right home, and there was no-one to contradict him, was there? But he couldn`t do it. That says it all, doesn`t it?"

"And then he made a run for it, the fool. He might have known that just doing that was enough to put his head in the noose."

"So what'll happen to him, then? Will Lord Sutton have to put the black cap on, or would it be Justice Livesey?"

"It won't be either them. They'll not do that here."

"I'll tell you what they'll do. They'll charge him, and then he'll be taken to Manchester and across the bridge to Salford Gaol. Then he'll have to go through King's Court, with a jury, but it'll not be much of an affair. The prosecutor will confront him with the evidence of his own admission, because it's no less than that, the jury will convict him, and it's then it'll be the time for the black cap."

"Is there no remission possible on account of her being, you know... what she was?"

"I think it might make a difference if it was somebody high born who did it, but not a weaver's lad."

"No chance of transportation, then?"

"I doubt it. If you ask me, it'll be the high jump."

"The drop," said someone else.

"The Tyburn Tree," said another.

"What do you mean, the Tyburn Tree, the Tyburn Tree's not in Salford, it's in London."

"No, but it's the same thing."

"How can it be the same thing?"

"I suppose you'd have to call it the Salford Tree, if you were going to call it a tree at all."

"Oh, never mind!"

"I'll say this, though," said one of the earlier speakers. "I wouldn't wish hanging on anyone, whether from a tree or a scaffold, or a yard-arm, or anywhere else, but if it has to be, I wouldn't have minded seeing the black cap, you know, here – in the Session room of the Old Boar's Head. The black cap, on the head of Justice Livesey."

"Eh, I'll tell you one thing, though..."

205

"What`s that?"

"They could never put the black cap on the head of Justice Gilbert. Why, his head would nodding so much, it`d fall straight off again, ha, ha, ha!"

"Ha, ha, ha!"

This was one everyone liked.

And it seemed that the night had now reached a point where each table in the room was finding something funny to share.

"Ha, ha, ha!"

They began to turn from one table to another, sharing their mirth, fellow to fellow.

"Ha, ha, ha! Ha, ha, ha!"

Locked in a room outside, behind the stables, with the constables guarding him, Simon put his hands over his ears, to exclude the laughter, which, in a dull form, he could hear nevertheless, and sitting on the rough bolster he had been given as a bed, rocked constantly back and forth.

In his room above, with access from the outside staircase, the young gentleman with the slight limp, who was now spending his third night at the inn, was composing a stanza, in the Spenserian form, about how the world would end, not in tears, but in a mad frenzy of hot-faced laughter.

"Ha, ha, ha!"

"Ha, ha, ha!"

Chapter 45

The weather had changed overnight. Gone was the bright sky and the bracing hint of autumnal frost; in their place, a shroud of wet mist hung over the hillside, half obscuring the church tower and causing an echo from Oliver Canky`s boot steps on the cobbles as he approached. He let himself in, and there was just enough grey light filtering in through the door for him to carry out his inspection. The cheeks, frequently ruddled, Canky suspected, with liquor, had started to take on a darker leathery appearance, and the lips were beginning to shrink back, revealing the teeth in death`s familiar rictus. She was all right for now, he reckoned, but if the weather was going to turn moist and warm, she was going to have to be despatched sooner rather than later.

There was an area in the graveyard, upheld by the parish, for paupers, and for those who had no-one to make arrangements for them and who`d made none for themselves, and such folk went in [and sometimes came out again] in their winding sheets, and with as few words as the Rector thought necessary for the inclusion of their miserable souls in the eternal roll call. In this case, though, there were the officials of the hearing, and possibly the Bamfords too to consider. Someone was going to have to make some decisions.

The inclement weather – for as the morning drew on, a steady drizzle set in – did not have any deterring effect on all those folk of the town who had got themselves up and ready early in order to make sure of getting a good seat in the Sessions room of the Old Boar`s Head, to witness the final scene of the drama which had been brimming up to a climax the previous day. By nine o`clock, an hour before proceedings were due to start, the room was full, and by half past, people were being asked to squeeze up along the benches which had been set for them. It had been a mistake, Will Robin, the landlord, now realised, to set a fire, as he had in the early morning chill, for the room was now already beginning to fill with the thick warm smell of damp garments giving up their moisture. He suspected that there would be another surge at the last minute, too, as soon as those still in the tap-room saw the magistrates making their entrance.

In this he was not wrong. The magistrates, and Lord Suffield, came to the table, and set out their books and papers, making ready, and the later arrivals from the public were ushered to standing positions along the back by the two constables, and an additional deputy who`d been sworn in for the occasion. Then a clear pathway was made so that the accused could be brought in.

Simon, white-faced and dishevelled, and with his hands tied behind, was brought in, to stand facing the bench. Around his eyes were smudges as if he`d been crying and the tears had been rubbed away by grubby hands or a piece of dirty sack. When the constables stepped aside, his knees seemed to give way, as if his own legs weren`t strong enough to hold him up, and for a moment, it seemed uncertain whether he would recover.

"Untie his hands," said Justice Livesey, "and bring him a chair to sit on."

There was a murmuring around the room as this was done, for it was seen that Sam Bamford had just come through the door, with one or two other newcomers, though not with Mima.

Lord Suffield`s cane brought the room back to order.

"Now, Simon," said Justice Livesey. "We have just one question to ask you, and it`s a simple one that you must answer truthfully, before God – did you, on the night before last, bring about, by battery, with or without malice aforethought, the death of Lucy Brindle?"

He had been thinking about this form of words since the previous evening, and had modified it several times, and several times again this morning. He judged now, however, from the rapt attention in the room, that he had struck exactly the right note of judicial authority.

The accused, however, had a strange look on his face, as if he had not expected the question at all, almost as if he had expected to be accused of something else.

They waited. He said nothing.

"Perhaps," suggested Lord Suffield, "he doesn't understand what you mean by *malice aforethought*. Try again."

"Simon," said Justice Livesey, now fearing for his judicial dignity, "did you murder Lucy Brindle?"

"Well?" said Lord Suffield.

"Well?" said Justice Tanner.

It was the nodding head of Justice Gilbert that seemed to persuade Simon, finally, that he must answer.

"No," he said.

There was now a muttering in the room, a disgruntled muttering, that carried with it a sense that Justice Livesey was letting the case slip. They had been prepared to feel sympathy for Simon, with his white and grubby tear stained face, but not for him to simply to deny it. To say no. Anybody could say no, when they'd been sitting there all night under lock and key and with the fear of the gallows to keep their eyelids from repose. Anyone could and would say no in those circumstances. What they wanted was someone who said yes. Did you kill Lucy? Yes, I did. That's what they wanted. That's what they expected. It was almost as if that was what they felt they deserved.

Lord Suffield now banged his cane sharply.

"Now listen to me, young man," he said. "You had the chance to exonerate yourself yesterday, and you didn't take it. You were asked if, after you'd been here you went straight home, and you didn't say, yes, that's what I did, I went straight home, which left us to surmise that you didn't. You were then asked what you did do, and still you refused to answer."

The room was now totally silent and gripped. If Justice Livesey didn't have it, Lord Suffield certainly did.

"So, I'm going to ask you again, what did you do when you left here? And don't try telling me now that you went straight home, because it won't do, I want to know exactly what you did do, so speak..."

"The boy's innocent," came a voice from the back of the room.

Every head turned.

What every head saw was a gentlemanly looking man, with curling auburn locks, and a handsome demeanour.

What the landlord saw was the gentleman with the limp who now owed him three, if not four night's rent.

What Lord Suffield saw was Lord Byron.

Who now stepped forward.

"There is no evidence to support a case against him."

"Have you followed the whole of this hearing, sir?" asked Justice Livesey, eager now to reassert, since Lord Suffield seemed, momentarily lost for words, his own authority.

"Enough of it to know that there is no case other than that of empty supposition. Besides," he added, "I can vouch for the boy."

"I think," said Lord Suffield, "that Lord Byron and I should have a word in private."

"There's no need," said Byron. "All I have to say may be said here in public."

"Let him speak," said Justice Livesey.

"I'm a paying guest at this establishment, have been for three days, the landlord will vouch for that. Prior to that I was a guest at Hopwood Hall. I came to stay here with a purpose to which Mr Gregge Hopwood is privy."

"Which was?" asked Justice Livesey.

"It had come to my attention, through Lord Suffield and others that there was unrest in the town over new machinery, as there is in Nottingham, my own part of the country. It is my intention to make a speech in the House of Lords when a bill, which has recently been proposed recommending the harshest of punishments for frame-breakers, as they are called, is read. I wished to be free to walk around the town, to listen to people, to be a fly-on-the-wall, in other words to make myself familiar with the thoughts and feelings of ordinary people."

"What, if I may ask," said Justice Livesey, "has this to do with the boy?"

"I'll come to that," said Byron, "but you asked me a question and I thought it deserved a fair answer."

"Very well."

"I was here two nights ago, and saw the boy come in. It was a few minutes after nine o`clock. He spoke to the landlord and then went to stand by the door, where he stayed for some time. Feeling pity for him, I took the trouble to ask what his errand was, and he told me. After that we fell into conversation."

"And what conversational topics," asked Lord Suffield, with some skepticism, "did you find in common with a fifteen-year-old weaver`s lad?"

"Precisely that," said Byron. "His master is a hand-loom weaver. There was a great deal he could tell me about the feelings of such men, the present hardships they endure, the fears they have as to what is to become of themselves and their families."

"And all this took place here, in the Boar`s Head?"

"No. The atmosphere here was somewhat boisterous, and becoming more so. We walked for a while through the town, and continued our conversation, for an hour maybe, and then I walked with him as far as to the door of his master`s house."

"Is this true?" said Justice Livesey, finding Simon where he had retreated, almost unnoticed, to a chair in the corner of the room.

The boy looked up and became conscious of all the eyes in the room now turning to him again. Then, almost imperceptibly, he began to nod his head.

"Say it," said Justice Livesey.

"Yes," said Simon, at last, "it's true."

"Then why did you not say so in the first place!" said Lord Suffield, rapping his cane angrily against the leg of the table.

"Perhaps," suggested Lord Byron, "he was afraid that he wouldn't be believed. Coming from him, uncorroborated, such a tale might have seemed a wild invention, more incriminating even than his silence. And if any man thinks it an easy thing to stand here, confronted by his accusers, and to keep a clear mind, then let him cast the first stone."

The room was silent. For the briefest of moments, Lord Byron's eyes met Simon's, and it seemed that the boy's expression was one of wry almost whimsical curiosity. Then, at a nod from Justice Livesey, Sam Bamford led him away to freedom.

"Thank you Lord Byron," said Justice Livesey, as the Sessions room crowd began to filter out in the direction of the tap-room.

Lord Suffield glared coldly.

"Your worship," said Oliver Canky, now coming forward, with his cap held to his breast with both hands. "If I might ask, sir, is it now fitting to make preparations for the poor girl to be decently buried?"

Chapter 46

It was a perfect night for the trade. Low cloud, with a hint of mist, the kind of autumnal mist that sometimes gathered over the river at night, providing the perfect camouflage.

Lucy Brindle had been buried that afternoon. The Bamfords had paid for a simple casket and for a short service in the church, and they had then stood, with Oliver Canky a respectable distance behind, by the graveside as the rector rehearsed the words of the committal.

"In hope of resurrection and eternal life..."

Was there the hope of resurrection, Canky mused, for the likes of Lucy Brindle? Unrepentant sinner that she was, did the likes of her still qualify?

If there was hope for the likes of Lucy Brindle, there was hope for everyone.

"Dust to dust."

Dust to dust, mused Oliver Canky, that sounded more like it. That was the bit of the liturgy that Oliver Canky recognised.

"From which it came, Amen."

Sam and Mima Bamford dropped, each of them, a small handful of earth onto the casket, in which, as they supposed, the mortal remains of Lucy Brindle lay. Only Oliver Canky, who had nailed down the coffin lid, knew that the funeral service had been, from start to finish, for the benefit of two sacks of cinders.

Ashes to ashes...

When they had retreated, in tearful consolation, Canky retrieved his shovel, discreetly concealed during the service, and filled in the hole with the clay and the loam which, by the sweat of his brow, he had dug out from it the previous day.

Then, his day`s work done, he went home to a nice veal pie which his Jenny-wren had made especially for him.

"You`ve taken it hard, this business, haven`t you? I know you have."

"It`s been having the body to look after, Jen. That`s what`s done it for me. That`s not a sexton`s business. That`s an undertaker`s business."

"Well, you`ve done what`s right, Oliver, and nobody can say you haven`t, so you just tuck into this nice veal pie I`ve made for you."

"It looks good, Jen. I always, say, you have the secret of making a veal pie better than anyone."

"You deserve it, Oliver."

"I`ll tell you something, though, Jen," said Canky, when he`d tested the veal pie and made his approval of it known, "I`ll not be fully happy until I`ve seen it through, good and proper."

"Seen what through, Oliver? What else is to be done?"

"Nothing but to keep a watch out, even if it`s just for one night, to make sure the grave isn`t violated."

"You do too much, Oliver!"

"I just follow my conscience, Jen, and if a man doesn`t do that, where does he stand? You don`t mind, do you?"

"I`ll not mind, Oliver, if you say I mustn`t, but I`m a bit sorry, because I was looking forward to wearing my green emeralds for you tonight."

There came the sound of a night bird from the church steeple as Oliver Canky opened his store. Inside, he noticed that the faint sickly odour he first detected in the morning had now grown, so that within a confined space it was now becoming more than unpleasant. God only knew what it must get like in those laboratories in Manchester where this secret and illegal work was done in the name of science. Still, they got used to it, he supposed. Men can get used to most things if they`ve got a reason for it.

214

By the light of a small candle, he finished stitching up the sheet with twine, and then blew out the candle, and sat to wait for Bill Nimmy and Sam Forcher.

He had wondered, going to see the man at Strangeways the previous day, if Lucy`s being a whore might put them off her, but it seemed not. Like Daniel, the crippled lad, every corpse had its use, it seemed. With Lucy, it might be the study of the pox, he speculated, or some other whorish indisposition, but it was all the same to him. What mattered was that the trip was on. Sam had said he`d help them as far as the river, but that he didn`t want the trip into Manchester, and so, this time, it was going to have to be himself and Bill.

After five minutes, he heard the signal, three brief curling whistles, and after another thirty seconds, as agreed, it came again, and he replied to it.

"Stand by the path, Sam. Bill, you help me out with her."

"It`s as dark as Hades in here, Canky. Can`t we have a candle for a minute?"

"No. Here, I`ll guide you to her feet. Once you`ve turned back towards the door you`ll make out the light from the dark."

"Going off a bit, isn`t she? Mind you, light as a feather, too. I`ll settle for that."

Taking it in turns to carry the body, they started off down the path towards the narrower ginnel winding round the edge of the Warren and past Canky`s house and yard. They moved, as ever, without speaking, slowly, picking their steps carefully, always alert.

"Stop!" said Bill Nimmy, after they had gone fifty yards, in a whisper so light it might have been the wind.

"What is it Bill?" asked Canky, in a similar whisper.

"I hear something."

They waited, stock-still, for ten seconds, twenty seconds, thirty seconds.

"Can you hear it still?"

"It`s the sound of a horse, hooves on stone, it must be up in the church yard."

They listened all three, attuning their ears.

"I can`t hear anything," said Canky.

"There`s a light," said Sam, suddenly. "Up there. It`s someone on a horse with a lantern."

They all looked back towards the church brow, where a small circle of orange light was already beginning to grow larger.

"He`s coming towards us. He must have seen us."

"Ssh!" said Canky.

"Let`s just let the body drop, and clear off out of here."

"Ssh," said Canky again.

Within twenty seconds, however, the horseman was upon them, holding his lantern aloft.

"What business is this?" he called, and they heard the drawing of a sword.

"Nothing, sir," Canky replied, recognising the voice of the man who had stood up to give Simon his alibi in the Sessions room of the Old Boar`s Head, the previous day; the man they had encountered once before whilst at the trade, and the man who, as Canky recalled, was less than a complete expert when managing his horse. "Nothing, sir. Just some woven cloth that has to be delivered, and that was not ready, with events in the town, until now."

"Let me see," said Lord Byron, holding his lantern closer. "Step into the light with what you`re carrying."

"Step forward, Bill," said Canky, at the same time drawing from his pocket the darning needle which he had used to sew Lucy up, and jabbing it sharply into the horse`s shank.

Whinnying, the horse reared sharply, and its rider tumbled off behind.

"Hurry on," said Canky to Bill and Sam. "Leave him to me. Wait for me at the bridge."

He grabbed the horse's reins to steady the creature, and then turned to the fallen nobleman.

"Sir!" he exclaimed. "Have you done yourself some harm? Can you stand? Take my arm and let me help you to stand."

"Let me sit for a minute," said Byron. "I'm shaken to pieces."

"Very well, sir. I'll stay with you until you're well enough to stand."

At last, with Bill and Sam now a good hundred yards ahead, he allowed Oliver Canky to help him to his feet.

"You're still shaky," said Canky. "My house is close by here. Let me take you there, so you can sit down and rest in a little more comfort until you're fully recovered."

With the horse's reins in one hand, and with the tottering lord on the other, Canky led the way to the bottom of the ginnel.

"Jen!" he called sharply. "Get down here straight!"

"What's this, Canky? And at this time of night!" she remonstrated, appearing from the stairs in her night attire, and sounding like one who was about to begin a shrewish fit.

"He's fallen from his horse," said Canky, "and needs some attention. Sit here, sir," he continued, leading the fallen horseman to the settee.

"Why, it's Lord Brian!" said Jenny Canky, now in a much mollified voice.

"I told you, he's fallen."

"Fallen," said Jenny, as if the word had a particular resonance for her.

"Don't just repeat what I said. Get a cloth with some cold water on it. We don't want him going into an apoplexy. Not here in our house."

"I'm all right," said Byron. "Just let me close my eyes for a minute."

"Just lie back and rest easy, sir," said Canky. "Let me take your boots off for you."

217

"No!" said Byron sharply, as if on that point, he was still entirely awake.

"Very well, sir, very well."

Reassured, as it seemed, Byron now closed his eyes, and seemed to lapse into a slumber.

"He`ll be all right now," said Canky. "When he wakes up, just tell him his horse is tied up in the yard."

"I will," said Jenny Canky. "I`ll tell him."

"I`ll get back there, then," said Canky, almost as a question.

"Yes, you get back there, Oliver. Don`t come back until you`re sure there`s no funny business going on. Don`t worry. I`ll keep a watch over Lord Brian, and I`ll send him off, on his horse, just as soon as he can manage it."

"You`re a good lass, Jen," said Canky.

"Am I?"

"You`re a treasure."

"Where am I?" said Byron, suddenly.

"It`s all right, sir," said Canky.

"I`m in agony."

"It`s all right, sir. Mrs Canky will see to you. She`ll make sure you`re all right."

After a moment, Byron slipped back into his slumber. Canky winked at Jen. "I`ll leave you to it then. Will you be all right?"

"I`ll do my best, Oliver. Come back in the morning, won`t you, safe and sound."

"Safe and sound," he promised. "Safe and sound."

When Lord Byron returned to consciousness and opened his eyes, the first image they found on which to focus was that of a row of green glass beads which caught the light of a nearby candle.

"They`re emeralds," said the owner of the invitingly fleshy, neck around which the beads were hung.

"Emeralds, are they, indeed!" said Byron, whose eyes, having now travelled a little way above the beads, and a little way below, found themselves not at all displeased by what

218

they saw. "And are you my ministering angel?" he added, noting the tenderness of care with which Jenny Canky was looking down at him.

"If I'm not mistaken," said she, "you were an angel once yourself, your highness."

"Indeed!" said Byron, intrigued.

"I recognised you straight away, your highness. It was your eyes..."

"My eyes?"

"Unmistakable. To me, anyway. And," she added, nodding in the direction of his legs, "if I'm not mistaken again, the reason you didn't want your boots removing is that you didn't want Canky to see anything in the nature of a cloven foot. Am I right?"

"How can I deny it?"

"So the old crone's prophecy was true after all!"

"Undoubtedly."

"Then what power have I..."

"None," said Byron.

"...to resist?" Mrs Canky concluded.

"None," Byron repeated. "None whatsoever."

Chapter 47

Two days later, at the request of his publisher, John Murray, who insisted that there were urgent matters to discuss, Byron returned to London. It was to be twelve years before his affairs in Rochdale were finally resolved, but Byron himself never returned to visit the Gregge Hopwoods, or Middleton, again.

After the release of Simon, and after Lucy Brindle`s obsequies, the search for her murderer proceeded no further, and within a few days it was replaced, in the gossip of the market place and the ale-house, by other topics. No-one was ever convicted of her murder, though of the four men linked with her and her last known movements - Skinner, Scrat, David Barton, and Simon - two of them knew whose hand it was that wielded the cudgel, and with what provocation the deed was done.

When news reached the Black Boy, in Manchester, of Lucy`s death, she was already a half-forgotten figure – for news travelled slowly and the world of the Black Boy was not, on the whole, one which cherished its memories for long. Whether Skinner had private thoughts of his own, regretful or guilty, at the news, he revealed to no-one, but to all intents and purposes, his existence as a fancy pal`s bully in the dark alleyways and courtyards of Manchester went on as usual. When, a year later, his body was found floating face-down in the Irwell, there were some people who said he`d jumped to his death from the Salford Bridge, with Lucy`s name on his lips, but it seemed more likely, as the authorities saw it, that he had simply met one of his own sort and had come off the worse for it. As had been the case with Lucy, there was little enthusiasm for following the matter up.

David Barton was seen less frequently in the drinking houses of Middleton than he had been before. He continued to work at his father's factory, though with no great progress, until the `events` of early 1812, and after that, declared his intention of studying for the ministry. He became an army chaplain in 1814, and died, along with a dozen other prisoners of war, of the typhus fever, in the gaol in Amiens two months before the defeat of Napoleon in 1815.

Owd Scrat continued his life in Middleton much the same way as he had before, attracting the same rumours as a nocturnal peeping Tom as he always had, but keeping his real secrets to himself – as he always had.

When Scrat's house was finally knocked down to make way for the new cemetery of Middleton and Thornham, on land purchased from the estate of Middleton Hall, the cellars were searched, prior to being filled in with rubble from the building itself, and nothing of any interest was found. Long before that, on the advice of Oliver Canky, to whom he had confided everything, and with his assistance, the partially embalmed body of Dorothea Edgeworth had been removed, in the dead of night, to a proper place in the old graveyard, though whether to its original resting place, or to another vacated in the line of Canky's trade is a matter of speculation.

And Simon simply disappeared.

It was a month after the trial, and one night he was there, and the next morning he was gone.

They searched high and low, and made enquiries in all the neighbouring parishes, but he was nowhere to be found. When Sam Bamford was reminded, by one or two who knew him well enough, that he had been something of an unpredictable rover at one time himself, anxiety for Simon passed gradually into the hope that he had gone off, as young men will, to make his way in the world.

It was two or three years later, on a visit to Manchester, and idling away some time until business resumed, that Sam

Bamford's attention was drawn, passing close by one of the old theatres, by the appearance of an uncommonly fine looking woman, and as men will, he stopped for a moment to admire. The woman was tall, exquisitely dressed in the fashion of the day, and had a proud bearing and demeanour, so that one might conjecture her, if not a lady of the highest breeding, an accomplished actress. As he watched, a carriage drew up beside her, and as a footman offered his hand to assist her, she turned, and as she did so, for an infinitesimal moment, their eyes met in recognition.

"Simon," he muttered to himself.

A moment later, the coach had driven away, and with it the illusion vanished. He stood, stock still, questioning the evidence of his own eyes, until at last a kindly passer-by stopped to ask him if he was quite well.

"Yes, thank you. Quite well."

"You looked as if you'd had a funny turn. Must be the heat."

"It's certainly a warm day."

"It is. Then good-day to you, sir."

"Good-day. Thank you."

It must have been the heat, Sam said to himself, as he continued with his business. By the time he was half way home, he had persuaded himself that his mind had simply played a trick on him. By the time he was home, he had all but forgotten about it.

True to his words in the Sessions room at the Old Boar's Head, on the morning when Simon was discharged, Byron went on to make his maiden speech in the House of Lords on February 16th, 1812. It was a passionate plea for greater understanding of the plight of those who saw their livelihoods threatened by new machinery. The Frame Work Bill, which proposed that frame-breaking should be treated as a capital offence, was passed in the Commons, and went into the Statute Book on February 27th.

It is quite likely that Byron would have been aware of the `events` in Middleton which happened on the 20th and 21st of April. A disorderly meeting in the town marched on Ezekiel Barton`s Mill, but was driven away by the mill`s workers, who, forewarned of the mob, had been supplied with fire-arms. Four of the rioters were killed, and on the following day, the mob marched again on the mill with whatever weapons they could find. This time they were dispersed by the Cumberland Militia, though some of the rioters made a diversion to Barton`s house, and set fire to it. There followed a night of chaos, with bonfires lit from furniture looted from the houses of mill workers; finally, and not without further bloodshed, the rioters were driven off by the militia and the Scotch Greys. It was one of several violent demonstrations that were to take place in Middleton in the coming decades.

Byron`s political career in England did not last long. The publication of `Childe Harold`s Pilgrimage` in the spring of 1812, took the literary world by storm, turning him into a cult celebrity who was worshipped and vilified, in equal measure, for the rest of his life. The unforgivable sin, a fashionable motif in some Romantic literature, which is the cause of Childe Harold`s melancholy wanderings, was never fully clarified, but it is thought by some modern commentators to be the act of sodomy.

Samuel Bamford went on to become a noteworthy figure in the wave of radicalism which spread, no less through Lancashire than through the country as a whole, in the dearth which followed the Napoleonic wars. After the massacre at St Peter`s Field, in Manchester, in 1819, one of the leaders of the peaceable crowd, he was pursued and imprisoned by the repressive authorities seeking to justify their own guilty actions.

The Anatomy Act of 1832, permitting the use of bodies, other than those who had been executed, for medical dissection, effectively brought to an end Canky`s trade, and the trade of many others like him, up and down the country.

Canky himself was sufficiently wealthy, when the old undertaker died, and with no-one in his family wishing to take it over, to buy the business, and thus to become a respected member of the community.

And as for Jenny Canky, she was happy to acknowledge, to herself, the continuing truthfulness of the prophecy once made by an old woman in the market place, for, nine months, almost to the day, since the night when poor Lucy Brindle`s body was ferried along the river Irk to Manchester, Jenny Canky was delivered of a son, healthy enough and like to live, which it did; and when, as the child grew, Canky himself referred to him affectionately as *the little devil*, she did not contradict him.

Not very long after Lady Mary`s death, Middleton Hall was demolished and the land sold to a railway company. The world was changing, and within half a century the sleepy rural township of Middleton had become unrecognisable, swept along in the furious flood-tide of new machinery and new markets. A hundred mills appeared, each with its own stack belching smoke into the sky, day and night, and then another hundred, drawing the townships of Middleton, Royton, Oldham, Rochdale and Chadderton, ever closer, as the *greensward and pastures sweet* of Samuel Bamford`s youth diminished year by year, forever.

In 1870, the huge Albany cotton mill was built where Middleton Hall once stood. Its address, with an almost perfect combination of respected tradition and utilitarian newness, was: 1, Old Hall Street.

The Albany Mill occupied the site for more than a hundred years, until the time came for another page in the history book to be turned. The site, once cultivated gardens and quiet orchards, next a constantly thrumming factory, is now occupied by the Middleton Arena, and is crossed by the dual carriageway which runs between the Oldham Road and the Rochdale interchange.

The end

Also by John Wheatley:

MARCIA, a Middleton novel – tells the story of a first-love that continues to haunt two people long after their lives have gone in different directions. Recording the rituals and intimacies of courtship and marriage, the novel evokes the changing faces of Middleton in the second half of the 20th century.

EVELYN, a Middleton novel - takes us back to the second world war and its impact on two Middleton families. Evelyn and Maureen, sisters-in-law, are drawn together when their husbands go away to serve. For Evelyn, the idyllic pre-war early years of her marriage are replaced the darkness and loneliness of separation. Both young women face conflicts and temptations, and in the aftermath of the war, both have hard decisions to make as they try to rebuild their lives.

John Wheatley`s Anglesey novels include:

A GOLDEN MIST
FLOWERS OF VITRIOL
THE WEEPING SANDS
THE PAPERS OF MATTHEW LOCKE
THE EXILE`S DAUGHTER

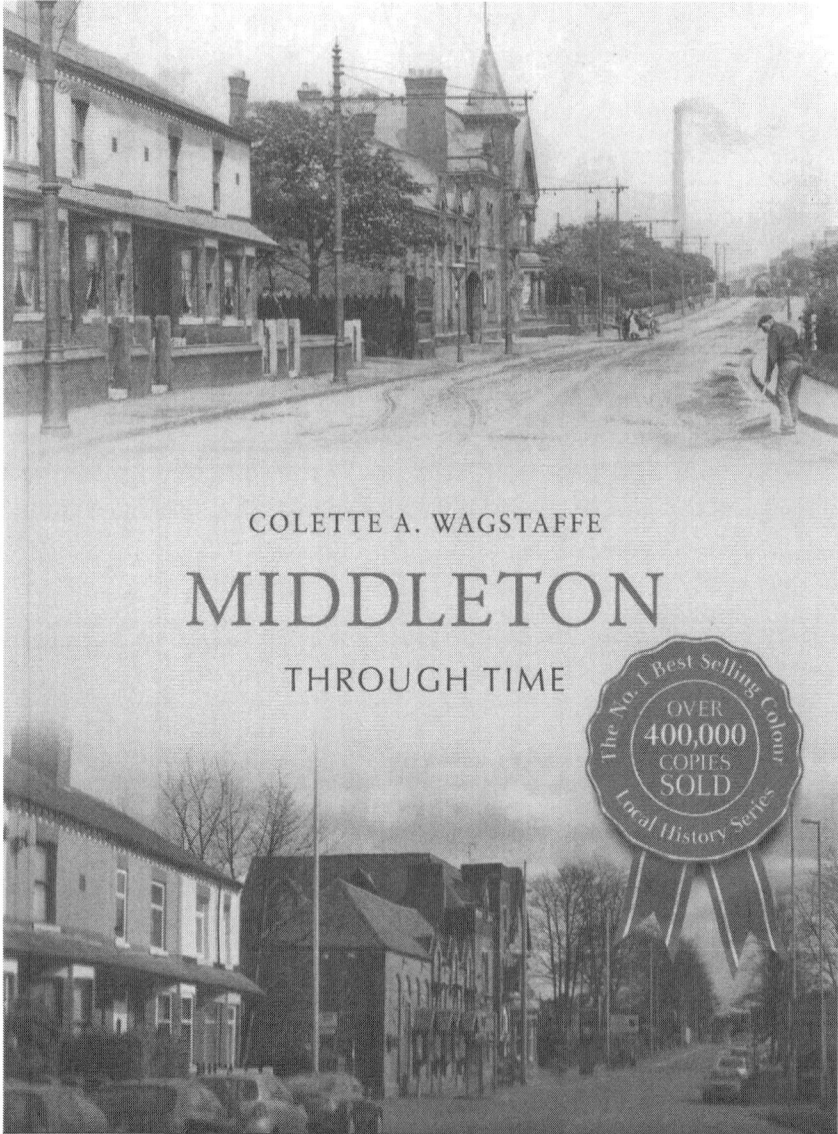

COLETTE A. WAGSTAFFE

MIDDLETON

THROUGH TIME

Printed in Great Britain
by Amazon.co.uk, Ltd.,
Marston Gate.